Frankly, My Detective

Frankly, My Detective

Mary L. Keeley

A Word with You Press
Publishers & Purveyors of Fine Stories in the Digital Age

www.awordwithyoupress.com

Keeley, Mary L.
Frankly, My Detective

ISBN-13: 978-0-9829094-5-4

Frankly, My Detective is published by:
A Word With You Press
310 East A Street, Suite B, Moscow, Idaho 83843

For information, please direct emails to: info@awordwithyoupress.com
or visit our website, www.awordwithyoupress.com.

Cover design by Teri Rider, teri@teririder.com
Interior design by Aren Ock, contact@arenock.com

Printed in the United States of America
10 9 8 7 6 5 4 3 2 1   17 18 19 20 21 22 23 24 25 26

A Word with You Press

Publishers & Purveyors of Fine Stories in the Digital Age

DEDICATION

With thanks and admiration to all the sassy, smart, strong, often mysterious women in those great old black and white movies thankfully still shown on TV.

Perhaps Richard Widmark described you all best when he said to Marilyn Monroe in *Don't Bother to Knock...*

"I can't figure you out. You're silk on one side
and sandpaper on the other."

❧❧❧❧❧

CHAPTER ONE

Life seems entirely different when you find yourself dangling from your seat belt because your car is upside-down.

She peered out at the topsy-turvy world and sighed.

"Well, here's another fine mess you've gotten us into," she muttered.

Fumbling, she managed to push the release button. The seat belt snapped, bounced off the steering wheel and whacked her hard on the chin.

"Ouch, damn it! Injury to insult or whatever!"

She pushed hard on the door handle and, just as she was squeezing out of the door, the airbag deployed with a harsh *whoosh, smack* and pushed her roughly out onto the glass spattered asphalt.

"Ummph! Ow!" she grunted as she was propelled onto her hands and knees, the glass pebbles digging into her flesh *and* her new jeans.

"Oh, great. Now you come popping out, you great lame marshmallow!" She tried to stand but her legs wouldn't cooperate. There were sirens, loud and close. Next minute strong hands were on her arms and legs dissuading her from trying to stand. Someone was asking her if she was okay.

"Well, not really. You see, I usually drive with the wheels on the ground." She herself was on the ground and it was hard and hot. The sun was in her eyes so she couldn't see who belonged to the voice over her head.

"Do you hurt anywhere?" the voice asked. She put up her hand in a feeble attempt to block the blinding late afternoon sun reflecting mirror-like off the water in Mission Bay.

"Nah, she usually administers the hurting." Now there was a voice she knew.

The paramedic leaned over her and two faces came into view. One was very cute indeed, dark hair, blue eyes, and nice teeth. The other face belonged to the voice she knew.

1

"Hey, Clifford, how's the cop business?"

"It'd be better if you stayed the hell out of it." Detective Clifford Dawson was squatting next to her, his large freckly hands dangling over the tops of his knees. The sun glinted off his bald pate making the last vestiges of red hair turn copper. He frowned down at her; he hated to be called Clifford, and she knew it.

"Jeez, Clifford, put a hat on, will ya? Your ugly head is blinding me!"

"Hey, do you mind? Trying to make assessment here." The very appealing paramedic was all business.

"I'm fine." She tried to get up, but strong hands pushed her easily back down on the ground. Her first instinct was to reach up and smooth her dark wavy hair, pushing it into submission. She'd used the good product this morning before she left home, but as her hairdresser reminded her, the hair always wins. Giving up on that, she tried to pull her hiked-up T shirt down over her waistband, making an attempt at modesty.

"You're not fine, until I tell you so. Now let me do my job, both of you."

"She's all yours, and good luck." Dawson stood up and backed off.

All questions asked and answered, she was strapped onto a gurney and bumped and bounced into the back of the waiting ambulance.

"Hey, I am seriously fine, I tell you. I don't need to go to any hospital. Just let me call and get a tow truck for my car and Uber for me and I'll be on my way, really. Clifford! Do something, damn it! Be useful for once!"

Dawson finished the conversation he was having with a highway patrolman and walked over to the ambulance. "Got what you need?" he asked the weary paramedic.

"Yeah, if she'll cooperate and give me her name. I take it you two know each other?" He waved his pen back and forth between the two of them, then held it poised over his clipboard.

"Why, Darlin', why won't you cooperate and tell him your name?" Dawson said, smirking.

"I told him to get it off my driver's license, but he doesn't want to wait for the fire guys to pry my bag out of my car. And he insists I give him my FULL name."

"So do it." There was that smirk again. "Or should I supply it for him?"

She pinched her lips together in a tight line. *Guess this is what I get for always calling him Clifford,* she thought. She watched him raise his eyebrows, turn to the paramedic and speak, emphasizing each word.

"The lady's full name is Scarlett O'Hara Butler Jane Eyre Salerno. She's a private dick."

Clearly confused, the paramedic looked back and forth between Dawson and the slightly disheveled dark-haired woman.

"Yeah, yeah. My mom is a book nut and she named me after her favorite literary characters, okay? Now you can laugh. *And* as for dicks...."

The paramedic snorted and coughed, trying to cover his laugh. Seeing the color rising on Dawson's face, he quickly put his head down, writing furiously on the clipboard.

"Her mama may be a book nut, but she's got nothing on her daughter. Talk with her a while and you'll find out; book nut or movie nut, still nuts. Now, Ms. Scarlett, wanna tell me what the hell you were doing chasing down *my* suspect?"

"Gosh, Clifford, wish I could, but you see, all of a sudden my little head hurts and I probably should go with luscious here and get checked out." She flashed a megawatt smile at the paramedic and gave him a completely un-shy wink.

"Yes, detective, if there's nothing else, we should get going," the paramedic said as he climbed into the rear of the ambulance.

Dawson began to protest, but the driver was already closing the doors.

As they closed, he heard Scarlett say as she wiggled her fingers at him, in her perfect Blanche DuBois, "Bye now. You know, I've always relied on the kindness of strangers."

"Why doesn't the Fire Department believe in shock absorbers for ambulances?" Scarlett asked the paramedic as they bounced and bumped off the shoulder and onto the road, the gurney's wheels protesting against the floor locks.

"Budget cuts."

"Very funny, doll face."

"Name's Trent," he said, pointing to his name badge.

"Short for Trenton? Were you born in New Jersey or was mom trying for something Hollywood-worthy?"

"Just Trent." He adjusted the bothersome neck brace he'd put on her earlier.

"Okay, just Trent, how soon can I get out of this joint?"

"Ms. Salerno, we're not even at the hospital yet! Why don't you try to relax and let me do my job?"

Scarlett saw the "all-business, I'm getting irritated" look on his face and sighed. She put her head back down on the paper-covered pillow and stared at the shiny metal ceiling. *Are those blood spatters up there?* She thought of asking, but Trent was busy talking with the hospital in some sort of medical-ese. She closed her eyes and tried to piece together just what had gone wrong with her latest investigation. How had she ended up with her sweet little sporty coupe upside down, her new jeans now grimy and not so fashionably ripped at the knees and her hands gravel-pocked, scratched and bloody?

It all started several months ago with a simple job. A hot-shit local businessman wanted her to spy on his boyfriend. But the client didn't want his trophy wife to know he had said boyfriend, who he was sure was cheating on him. What he didn't know was the trophy wife had ALSO hired Scarlett to spy on her husband so she could prove he'd broken their pre-nup. Scarlett was good at her job AND being careful, so she successfully kept each party in the dark about her working for both of them. The complication started when the businessman showed up dead---really dead. We're talking *Rasputin* dead. Poor bastard had been poisoned, shot, stabbed and finally drowned in his own marble Jacuzzi. Somebody wanted this guy seriously gone.

And now both the boyfriend and the trophy wife were AWOL. The car Scarlett had been chasing was the wife's, but the wife wasn't the driver. Scarlett didn't know who it was, but suspected the silver BMW had been stolen by the boyfriend. Clifford the cop had been tracking down the wife, who had very inconveniently disappeared. Of course, Clifford didn't like Scarlett interfering, so she didn't tell him she was on the case. Her secret source in the department kept her aware of Clifford's investigation, enabling her to dodge him and the rest of the San Diego PD. The blond, wavy-haired boyfriend was set up in a nice little condo in the Mission Hills area. It wasn't hard to stake out this guy or even follow him. Scarlett thought he might be clueless, or perhaps he just wanted to appear that way. She had suspected he was the killer at first, but that didn't make sense. The guy wouldn't off his meal ticket and neither would the wife.

Despite the discomfort of the gurney. Scarlett smiled. Clifford didn't know about the boyfriend. Some detective he was. He was chasing the car because he thought the wife was driving. Scarlett knew she wasn't, for one simple reason: she knew where the wife was.

"I'll get you, my pretty, and your little dog, too," she murmured.

"What was that?" Trent asked.

"Pay no attention, cute Trent. It's just a habit of mine."

"To talk in movie quotes? Why?" He frowned down at her, checking her pulse once again.

"Makes my life easier. Don't have to be original all the time." They pulled up to the Sharp Hospital Emergency Room entrance. As Trent and his partner pushed the gurney into the ER, Scarlett looked around and sighed, "What a dump!"

"Bette Davis in *Beyond the Forest* and how are we today, Ms. Scarlett?" The tall, white-coated doctor took the chart from the grateful paramedic and smiled down at her.

Scarlett smiled back. "Ah, Doc, always good to trade quotes with you. I'm fine, really, just need to blow this joint."

"Well, m'dear, don't be so anxious. Gotta check you out. Came back down here as soon as they radioed ahead it was you. *Again!*" He shook his head and clucked his tongue in mock reprimand. He leaned down and looked at her bloodied knees, palms and elbows.

"My, my my my my. What a mess." He placed his stethoscope in his ears but before he could place it on her chest, she grabbed it and spoke into it.

"Tommy Lee Jones in *The Fugitive;* great performance, got an Oscar, I believe. Good quote but you can't beat me at this, Doc. Your joint smells like alcohol and not the good kind."

He yanked the stethoscope away from her, frowning.

"Get serious for a second,, will ya??" He turned and barked orders in medical alphabet soup at a giggling nurse's assistant, then resumed examining the impatient Scarlett. "What the hell were you doing this time? Paramedics radioed you flipped your car." He shone his penlight in her eyes. Apparently satisfied with what he saw or didn't see, he straightened and raised his dark eyebrows at her, waiting.

Scarlett sighed and leaned back on the pillow, closing her eyes. Her head was beginning to hurt for real now.

"I was on a job, okay? You know I can't tell you more than that, Evan. Is Cat on duty?"

Evan returned the sigh as he checked her pulse once again. "Yep, she's on duty in the NICU. I'll page her right now. Just wanted to make sure you weren't terminal or anything. Let's get you cleaned up a bit." He reached for the page-phone by her bed. Scarlett sat up suddenly.

"Oh, let me page her, please, please!" Evan pushed her away with one hand, holding the phone with the other.

"Not on your life! You'll use her full name and she'll be pissed at *me* for letting you." The curtain of the cubicle was pulled back suddenly.

"Knock it off, you two. This is a hospital, after all." The nurse wore blue scrubs and had a brightly colored NICU identification tag around her neck.

"Hey, there's my wonderful Catherine ...." Before she could finish, the nurse came inside yanked the curtain closed and growled at her. Her expression was as serious as Scarlett's wasn't, but the family resemblance and attitude were unmistakable.

"Don't finish Scar. I'll level you or inject you with something horrible, I swear." Cat's amber eyes met her sister's dark green ones and looked menacingly feral; then her voice softened as she came to her sister's side. "Are you okay, or just a major nuisance as usual?"

"Ah, you found out I was here all on your own. The moors and I will never change. Don't you, Cathy." Scarlett smiled wickedly at her sister.

"Cut it out, Scar. Don't quote Heathcliff to me. Answer me like a real person!" She was clearly irritated.. Scarlett sighed and acquiesced.

"Fine, really Cat. Just some scrapes. Car's a mess, though. Don't call Mom; I'll be out of here as soon as somebody lets me go." She cast a withering look at Evan. He made some sort of grumpy noise in his throat.

"Yeah, she checks out fine. Just ordered some preliminary labs and we'll clean up her boo-boos and she'll be home for dinner. No need to upset Rosa." He made a kissing mouth at his wife, thumbed his nose at Scarlett and left.

"God, Scar, why don't you quit this shitty business and use your degree to teach or work as a public defender or something. This is the third bad scrape this year. Don't you think the odds …?"

"Catherine, the odds have been against me from the beginning. How many successful female private detectives, are there in the real world anyway? Why can't you be proud and supportive of me? Oh, yeah, I know why. 'Cause I refuse to be like you and get a girly job." Scarlett pulled her hand away from her sister's and folded her arms across her chest, immediately regretting diminishing Catherine's very difficult job. Catherine sighed.

"Scar, you play that 'I gotta be me' tune all the time. Nobody buys it anymore."

"It worked fine for Sammy Davis, Jr."

Cat leaned over the bed rail fixed her eyes on her sister's. "We all— me, Evan and Mom— just want you to stop taking so many risks. Why can't you understand we want you to be safe?" Her voice rose despite the control she tried to maintain and she self-consciously put her hand over her mouth.

Scarlett put both hands on the bed rail and leaned over, speaking to her sister in a hoarse whisper.

"O.K. Cat, I get it, but the problem is *you* don't. None of you. This is a big case, worth a lot, and I'm the only one with a good hold on it. Me. Not the cops, not any other detective. Me, Cat, and I'm within a gnat's eyelash of solving it. When I do, there's a pile of money in it. Enough to take care of Mom the way she should be, you know? I can help! I want do that, Cat."

"Scar, we can take care of Mom. But you know that's not it. You want, I don't know, the gory glory of it all. I just don't get it."

"You think I don't know how much you and Evan have in student loans? Not to mention some of my own debts. Let me solve this big one and we'll all be in the black. No more judgments, huh, Sis?"

A nurse came in with a wound kit.

"Call me when you get home, okay? AND my job is anything but 'girly'!" Cat said emphatically as she pulled the curtain back.

"Do you know her?" the nurse asked as she opened the wound kit.

Scarlett looked up at her with a look of astonishment and spoke loudly, delighting in how her sister's shoulders hunched at her words.

"Why? Don't you? She's the famous Catherine Earnshaw Holly Golightly Salerno O'Malley. Talk at ya later, Cat!"

Catherine groaned and without turning gave Scarlett the famous one-fingered salute.

The firefighters returned Scarlett's purse to her before she left the hospital and since Evan was going off duty anyway he drove her to the car rental office. She patiently put up with the same "get out of this business" lecture from him, thanked him with a sisterly peck on the cheek. When he drove away, she sighed and gratefully turned the key in the nice little Toyota rental. She wound her way down University Avenue past all the new coffee shops, restaurants and trendy boutiques that were part of the revival of her North Park neighborhood. Soon she was at the front door of the small, pre-war bungalow she owned not far from Morely Field. It was a sweet little stucco number, built along the quiet wide streets just north of Balboa Park. The little homes had been residents of the many military and defense industry families before WWII and had stayed consistently occupied over the years, even when the larger suburbs built east and west of the city developed. The area had become a bit run-down, some streets bearing the look of "progress" over the years, which simply meant lovely old houses were torn down and apartment buildings were crowded in between the bungalows and the Craftsman homes of the last century. Smart investors and people seeking the quaint neighborhoods, larger lots and solid construction of the older homes had moved back into the area in the last few years. University Avenue and El Cajon Boulevard began to spruce up with new businesses taking over the old JC Penney building which now housed Wang's North Park, an upscale Asian fusion restaurant whose excellent Happy Hour fare had called to out Scarlett many times. Even the old Woolworth and Lerner's department store buildings had been converted to antique malls boosting their prices by labeling their inventories "vintage." Scarlett was lucky to have purchased her little home just before the real estate upswing took over North Park and she smiled as she pulled into her long driveway, got out of her car and saw the wide, arched front porch of her white-stucco abode.

The house was dark and she instinctively reached in her purse and closed her hand over her gun.

"It's me," she called out as she put her hand up to feel for the wall switch. "It's Scarlett. Meet me in the kitchen."

She stood in the living room and waited. The house had a small door leading from the living room to a hallway. A door at the far end of the hallway opened up shining a small shaft of light on the old telephone niche in the wall beside the bathroom. The door was open, but no one came out.

"Seriously, it's okay. Are you hungry? I'm starved. How about some pasta with broccoli, garlic and Romano cheese, maybe some red pepper flakes? Sounds good, huh? Come on, you set the table and I'll cook." Scarlett walked through the arched opening to the dining room, shedding jacket and purse. Shoving her gun into the back waistband of her jeans, she winced at the pain in her bruised shoulder.

The spare bedroom door opened all the way and a small figure walked slowly from the hallway into the kitchen. She hugged her arms about her as if she were freezing, despite the warmth of the late summer night.

"Do you have some wine to go with the pasta?" she asked.

"Red or white. Which one do you prefer?"

"I think white tonight."

"Got a great Pinot Grigio right here for you." Scarlett reached in the refrigerator, pulled out the bottle, opened it quickly and poured it into two juice glasses sitting on the drop-leaf kitchen table. She held one out to her guest. Scarlett did have nice wine glasses, but using juice glasses was something her Sicilian Dad had always done and she liked remembering him that way. The two women sipped quietly for a moment.

Scarlett went to the stove, turned up the heat on the pasta water and said, "So, dear, how was your day?"

"Did you get him?"

"Not today, but I will, soon."

"I hope you're right," the trophy wife said and drained her glass.

CHAPTER TWO

Scarlett ran the last piece of rigatoni around the inside of her pasta bowl, soaking up the last bit of olive oil and melted Romano cheese. She popped the bite in her mouth, closed her eyes and sighed with pleasure. A mirthless laugh from her dinner companion caused her to open her eyes and frown.

"What's up? Want dessert? I've got some great gelato from the place out in Little Italy. You know, Pappalecco's out there off India on State. Best gelato outside of Florence."

"Good God, no! Bad enough you've got me eating carbs again, now you want to feed me sugar *and* dairy?" With that, Lizette Tangerine Yokum Di Stefano pushed back her bowl as if it were a live, crawling thing and grabbed the wine bottle. She filled her glass for the third time, leaving a scant trickle for her hostess.

"Oh, I see, pasta and gelato bad; alcohol good?" Scarlett raised an eyebrow at Lizette's bowl. The broccoli was gone but most of the delicious pasta remained. Looking down at her own empty bowl, she sighed.

"Yeah, well, being Italian, I never met a carb I didn't like, unfortunately." She silently reminded herself to not get on the scale after a pasta dinner and to check in her closet for clean workout clothes. Putting the wine bottle neck up to her eye, she squinted at the meager contents before she shook the last drops of the Pinot Grigio into her own glass. They drank in stony silence for a while. Scarlett spoke first.

"Look, Lizzie, I gotta move you, the cops know I'm on the case and they'll be watching me now."

"Where'm I supposed to go? And stop calling me Lizzie—it's Lizette or maybe even Mrs. Di Stefano to you. You work *for* me, remember?" Her heavily black-lined grass-green eyes flashed with anger. Not for the first time Scarlett looked at her charge and thought with those eyes and that deeply

9

dyed black hair Lizette seriously looked like a deranged Halloween cat.

"Hey, don't get your skinny little back up. I'm protecting you, remember? The cops think you're a prime suspect in dear old Sebastiano's demise. And since you and I are the only ones who think we know who did the deed you'd best do as I say until I catch the bastard, or whoever got hired to do the hit, right? You should know me by now. 'I've always wanted to fight a desperate battle against incredible odds.'"

Lizette gave her a look that said, "What the hell?"

Scarlett exhaled, with intent. "It's a quote from a movie, *The Last Starfighter*. Honestly, have you ever seen anything besides those cheesy vampire movies? Just be patient a bit longer, my pretty, and you'll soon be the rich-bitch widow you've every right to be. *Capito?* Now go pack your beauty trunk while I do the dishes and we'll be outta here in no time. Clear your place, will ya?"

Ignoring Scarlett's reproof, Lizette picked up her bowl and glass and put them on the counter next to the sink with a careless "clink."

"Look, I just don't want to end up like one of Cosmo's little slaves, ya know? I mean his whole operation, it's so messed up. I hired you to protect me, and get what's mine, so I gotta be sure, get it?"

"You'll be safe, Lizzie. I mean, have I ever lied to you before, huh?"

"Is that some other kinda movie quote or are you for real this time; it's hard to tell." With that, she left the room in a huff, her slim hips moving in an angry sway made perfect with practice. She'd been a model, if you want to call working shopping mall fashion shows and posing next to new cars on turntables at fairs and car shows modeling. At her moderate height, she really didn't qualify for the big time. But she looked fantastic in a bikini, thanks to her saving all through her waitressing teen years for a great boob job.

It all paid off when she was seen at one of the infamous car shows, lounging sexily on the hood of a red Ferrari by none other than Sebastiano Andrea Di Stefano, successful import/export business owner.

Yano, as he was called, liked fast cars and dark-haired women who were blissfully endowed. And so, the match made in heaven, or at least in the Presidential suite of the historic Hotel Del Coronado, was made legal and binding, oh so binding, just two short years before Yano's unfortunate demise. Sadly, for Yano anyway, besides liking women, he also had a distinct affection for muscular, blond, long-legged young men.

Yes, Scarlett thought now as she rinsed the dishes and put them in the dishwasher, Yano had lots of likes and even yens when it came to both sexes. But something he never seemed to have, despite his money and the power that came with it was: trust. Yano had not trusted Lizette and he had trusted his boyfriend, Jordan Blakely even less.

Scarlett had seen this so many times when it came to romance, lust, whatever you called it. Whether the relationship was totally legal or miserably clandestine, nobody trusted anybody.

"And that's why you are still single, Scarlett, baby," she said out loud to herself as she put the clean pasta pot away. "And that's why you're gonna stay that way, and that's why business is good. Let'm live, love and betray each other. What the hell, it pays my bills!"

She turned out the lights in the kitchen, took out her gun, made sure the safety was off and grabbed her purse and keys.

"Come on, Lizzie. Shake a tail feather, we're outta here!"

The drive didn't take long. It was a quiet night on Hwy 8 West, for a change.

"We're going to the beach?" Lizette asked warily peering out the car window and ducking her head when a car passed.

"Near the beach. Not the snooty one you're used to, Lizzie. We're headed to one of the best beach towns in San Diego, maybe in all of California, in my humble opinion, of course." Scarlett gave a short laugh as she saw the frown barely forming on Lizette's Botoxed forehead. "No worries, it's not a dump or anything where I'm taking you. The neighborhood's old and slightly funky, but you'll like the place. The owner is a real class act and the best cook in the world. Again, just my opinion and nothing humble about it this time." She stopped at the light on Sunset Cliffs Boulevard and looked up and down the side streets lined with old stately palm trees. She pointed to the stucco building set deeply into the west corner of Santa Monica Ave.

"That's the most charming of the San Diego Public Libraries. Not huge, but so cozy and welcoming. Ever been in a library, Lizzie?" Her voice was gently teasing.

"Humph! Of course I have! Had to get through high school somehow didn't I? Certainly weren't any fashion or movie magazines around our crummy house, let alone books."

"Well, all righty then. It's been established, you done been educated, after a fashion. Pun intended, Lizzie." The light changed and Scarlett turned left and they drove up the steep hill in chilly silence.

The driveway was nice and wide and the only light in the house was shining dimly through the heavy, drawn drapes of the large front window. Scarlett blinked her headlights twice as she pulled the car up close to the hedge beneath the window. Within minutes, the porch light came on, went off and came on again. The signal was an old one, but known only to Scarlett and the woman inside and always reliable. Scarlett got out first, gun in hand, and checked the darkened street before she signaled Lizette to get out and follow her. As soon as her foot hit the small stoop, the front door opened and they were inside, door locked and porch light out. It took all of less than 15 seconds.

"Get in, get in, you're making me miss my stories!" The small white-haired woman in the rose-colored robe and matching slippers fairly pushed them from the entryway into the dimly lit living room. A large television in an old console cabinet bore the scene of an impossibly handsome man and a stunningly beautiful woman engaged in a heated argument that soon melted into a soggy embrace accompanied with slurpy kissing sounds.

"Oh, now, see, I'm missing this!" The woman shuffled over to the console, putting on the glasses she held. "Now, wait, wait, I think I know how to turn this off or is it 'pause' I want? Oh, Honey, help me!"

"It's 'pause'. Here, I've got it." Scarlett was across the room in an instant and pushed the button on the old VCR atop the console. The little woman straightened and sighed.

"Oh, good, now I can catch up." She turned to Scarlett. "You're here late. I thought you'd be here earlier. I've made Cannoli."

"Sorry, couldn't be helped. Here, let me introduce you to your new caregiver."

"Now Scarlett, you know I don't need anyone like that!" The woman drew herself up to her full five-foot height and shook her finger under Scarlett's nose.

"I know, but that's what we gotta say for now, o.k.? Just play along like usual, right?"

The older woman smiled and took Scarlett's face in her two small but pretty hands and patted both cheeks. "All right, my little snoopy pants, all right, I'll cooperate, like usual."

They both laughed as Scarlett took the hands from her face and still holding them turned to a very puzzled Lizette and said, "Lizette Tangerine Yokum Di Stefano, I'd like you to meet Rosa, your patient for the next few days."

Rosa freed her hands, came to Lizette and pulled her into a fierce embrace that belied her apparent frailty. She stood back, her hands on Lizette's stick-thin arms, squeezing them hard, oblivious to Lizette's wincing.

"I'm…it's good to meet you. Shall I call you Rosa?" Lizette stammered.

"Oh, no, *Bella Mia*, you just call me what Scarlett does: Mama!" Leading the way into the kitchen, she continued, "Scarlett, Honey, put your nasty gun away and let's get this thin little girl some Cannoli!"

❦❦❦❦❦

"And so, Honey, why the middle moniker 'Tangerine'? Not that I mind, ya know, love really different names myself." Rosa winked at Lizette as she busied herself at the kitchen counter filling the Cannoli shells.

Scarlett leaned against the opposite counter, waiting for the decaf to brew. At Rosa's last statement she rolled her eyes at Lizette.

Clearly uncomfortable, Lizette cleared her throat and replied: "My Dad loved the stupid old song, *'Tangerine, she is all they claim.'* I remember him coming home with a snoot full and singing it to me and Mom. He's the one responsible for the weird name. Wanted it for my first name, but Mom won out, one thing I can thank her for, I guess. And Scarlett's name is from that Civil War old movie, huh. Book, too, I think. See, I know stuff." She flashed a quick, sharp look at Scarlett, shrugged and sat at the dining room table which Rosa invited her to with a gesture.

"So, didn't get along with Mom or Dad, I guess? How sad, huh, Scarlett, Honey. Family is so important; everything really." Rosa shook her head sadly as she brought the plate of cannoli over to the table. "Now, a little dessert always helps. Right?"

"MMMMMM." Scarlett poured the coffee and smiled at the always carefully laid table as Rosa dished up the cannoli. The plastic placemats decorated with grape clusters were placed on the thick table pads that covered the maple tabletop. In the center of the table was a circular crocheted cloth. Scarlett brought it back as a gift for Rosa from her solo trip to Italy after law school. Her mother treasured it. A beautiful *Deruta Ceramica* bowl sat atop the cloth, an heirloom from Rosa's own grandmother. Scarlett and her sister Cat had often remarked they could count on their eyeballs the times they'd seen the lovely table top without its protective pad. Rosa would dismiss their good natured teasing with the same statement: "Your daddy worked hard to give us nice things. Gotta work to keep 'em that way."

"Don't be shy, Lizette, dig in," Scarlett said.

"Um, what's in the filling, can I ask?" Lizette eyed the powdered and filled pastry tube on her plate as if it were about to attack her.

"Oh, my usual. Ricotta, a little mascarpone, almond flavoring, some chopped up chocolate and almonds, a little cinnamon. Try it."

"Sugar?" Lizette asked timidly?

"Oh no! Never. It would make the whole filling grainy and much too sweet."

Lizette smiled gratefully, cut a small piece and took a bite. Her eyes opened wide as combination of flavors and textures caressed her taste buds.

"My God this is so good! Are you sure there's no sugar? It's so rich."

"Oh no, Dear, just a little honey to help it along. Makes the filling so much more smooth, don't you think?" She took a generous bite of her own cannoli.

Scarlett herself was chewing her cannoli with relish, her eyes closed in rapture. Lizette's choking brought her back to reality. Rosa was up out of her chair, clapping the young woman on the back with such force, Lizette's face was nearly in her plate.

"What's up, Lizzie, go down the wrong pipe?"

Lizette wiped her eyes with her napkin. "Honey? And the Ricotta, that's dairy, right?" She croaked, turning to glare at Scarlett.

"Relax, Lizzie, just give in to life's little pleasures won't ya? You know, it isn't only the big ticket items in life that make you happy. 'Leave the gun. Take the Cannoli.' Good advice, right, Mama?"

Rosa smiled and nodded, "Sure, *Bella Mia*, can't argue with that."

Lizette sat with her hands gripping the edges of the table, looking from Scarlett to Rosa who continued to chat and eat as if she wasn't there. Finally, she sighed loudly, looked down at her plate, picked up her fork, cut a good-sized bite and said, "What the hell?" Her eyes closed as she slowly surrendered herself to the joy of a great cannoli.

Later, while Scarlett washed the dishes, Rosa showed Lizette the rest of the house ending up in the frilly blue and white bedroom that Scarlett and Catherine had shared. "So Sweetie, any questions for me?" Rosa tilted her head and asked with a warm smile.

Lizette took a deep breath before asking. "So how come you help Scarlett and for how long? I mean, she good at it and nice and all, but being a PI is a creepy business isn't it? Do you like what she does?"

Rosa sighed and sat down on one of the perfectly made twin beds and gestured for Lizette to sit opposite her on the other. "Five years ago Scarlett came over and showed me her brand new private investigator's license. I looked at the piece of paper in her hand for a long time, saying nothing. When I finally looked up at my daughter I was in tears." Spreading her small hands and raising her shoulders, she continued with her narrative.

"'Ah, *Bella Mia*'," I said, "'why this, huh? Why do you want to meddle in other people's business?' And you know what she said?"

Lizette shook her head, waiting. Rosa smiled and continued.

"Well, first, Scarlett laughed so hard we both ended up crying! But she explained to me that her vision of the job was more helping than meddling and the money could be good. Well, I have to admit it took a few months of talking over many dinners. You know how it's always easier to talk when there was food around, right?" She ignored Lizette's shrug and continued.

"So I began to understand why Scarlett wanted this. I was so proud when Scarlett finished law school." Rosa sighed again.

Lizette nodded. "So, yeah, I know she's a lawyer, but why she doing this stuff? I mean the lawyer pay is off the hook, right?"

Rosa nodded and continued. "My Scarlett is one smart cookie, but face it, she got tired and not a little disgusted by being the low-on-the-totem-pole girl at the law firm. It just wasn't her style to do all the leg work and not get the credit or the money the senior lawyers and partners got. She's too independent for that and who knows, maybe I knew that better than anybody."

Rosa stood up and went over to the large dresser and looked for a quiet moment at Scarlett's college graduation picture. "Still, it was a while before

Scarlett became known as a reliable, ethical investigator. The people, the clients, who came to her learned pretty quickly she could protect them and their 'interests' even if it meant they had to disappear for a while."

Rosa turned back to Lizette and smiled and pointed to herself. "That's where Mama came in. At first, ya know, I was pretty skittish and reluctant about having strangers in my house; it's my nest, right?" Rosa smiled and gave a short laugh. "I keep my house, well, like I was taught, tidy, and no clutter. Some smarty pants members of this family refer to it as a museum."

Lizette looked around and the impeccable room and its attention to detail. The simple light fixtures, the tidy dresser adorned with family pictures, including Scarlett's and Cat's graduation pictures from both high school and college, small religious statues and lovely pieces of Italian blown glass. Lizette smiled and nodded her understanding. She turned as Rosa continued.

"But I don't care, I take pride in my house and my appearance *and* both my daughters' accomplishments. Either one asks for my help, well, I'm their Mama after all, so I help. Anybody Scarlett brings, I treat like family and I try to help her get them going in the right direction. You see?"

Lizette stood and walked over to Rosa. Wrinkling her forehead as much as the Botox would allow, she nodded and said, "Yeah, I see. And you know what, Mrs. Salerno? Scarlett and her sister are damned lucky to have you. I know from experience, moms like you are pretty rare."

Rosa grinned and pulled Lizette into another nearly crushing hug. "Aw, that's so nice of you to say, Sweetie. I know we're gonna get along just fine." She pulled back and looked Lizette up and down, raising her eyebrows at the trendy designer clothes her new charge was wearing. "Okay, let's get started at making you look like something you're not." With that, she took Lizette's hand and pulled her over to the large closet and pushed open one of the mirrored doors.

So now Lizette was to be dressing in the dowdy clothes provided, wear no make-up, pull her dark tresses back in a ponytail and pretend to be invisible. That way, if any of the neighbors happened to see her, she could be explained away as a companion or a distant cousin from Italy who spoke no English; whatever Rosa wanted her to be, it didn't matter. The only thing that mattered was that Lizette was safe and that neither the police nor the man who wanted to kill her would find her.

⁂

At the front door, Scarlett reminded Rosa to use only the pre-paid "burner" cell phone provided for the times when they needed to make their conversations as private as possible, as they usually did when they were protecting someone. Scarlett always told Rosa the people she brought to her were to be protected— she couldn't bring herself to use the word "hidden",

15

even though they both knew that's just what they were doing: hiding someone.

CHAPTER THREE

Driving down Sunset Cliffs Boulevard north over the bridge on her way towards her next stop in another beach community, Scarlett's mind drifted once again to the next player in her current drama: Cosmo.

Cosmo Dante Di Stefano, Yano's Uncle and titular head of the family business hated his nephew and the *puttana* he married. If he didn't find her and kill her, his nephew's money would go to her instead of him. Not the worst thing, even though Cosmo had more money than God, he always wanted more. The worst thing: he thought of his *pazzo* nephew as a stupid fag not even smart enough to successfully hide his secret relationships from Cosmo's troops. He'd had Yano tailed for a long time, had bugged both his fancy house and his not-so- secret city condo. He knew about the boyfriend, that condo he'd set him up in and the credit card accounts Cosmo had lavished on both the boy-toy and the stupid excuse for a wife. Cosmo had even known for a time about the supposedly secret deals he had with certain Vegas "businessmen." And if he lacked the brains to hide *these* parts of his useless life from his uncle and his sources, it would surely get out to other "business" associates. Cosmo couldn't have that happen. He would not be disgraced by association.

"And the bastard has a mole in the police department," Scarlett said aloud as she sat at the stoplight. "So, Ms. Salerno, you'd better move fast, 'cause between the cops and Cosmo, you and Lizzie could be seriously dead. "'Fasten your seat belts, boys and girls. It's going to be a bumpy night!'"

✿✿✿✿✿✿

The cell phone's ring made him jump and spill his drink on the red-checked paper place mat. Several heads turned towards his booth at the loud rendition of *Heroes,* his ring tone. Normally he loved the David Bowie song but today he with all he had on his mind, it was an irritation. He picked up the phone quickly and turned to face the wall as he answered, his back hunched over, hoping no one could hear his conversation.

"Where the hell are you? I've been out of my skin waiting." Jeremy Blake's normally deep voice sounded harsh even to him. The voice on the other end of the call sounded calm and confident, but not reassuring.

"Don't get your panties in a wad, Sweetheart, just tell me where you are."

Jeremy turned to look over his shoulder and said in a hoarse whisper, "I'm at a restaurant that a friend owns here in Hillcrest. What's happening? What am I supposed to do now? You said I'd be safe if I did what you wanted. The cops almost got me!"

A deep chuckle from the caller. "Listen, there's no time to panic now, we're close to getting you what I promised. Where's the car? You didn't leave it on the street did you?"

"No, it's behind the restaurant in the alley between two big dumpsters. I thought it would stay kinda hidden that way."

The caller gave a low whistle. "Wow, curly top, I'm a bit, not a lot, but a bit impressed. Good thinking. Now it won't stay hidden for long, so here's what you do next. Wait till dark, smear some mud or something on the back license plate so it can't be seen clearly and drive the car up to the Off Hwy 8 Motel in Pine Valley. Get a room and stay there until I call."

Jeremy began to sputter, "I can't do that, I don't have a bag packed, I don't have a change of clothes, and I don't have my THINGS!"

"Oh put a cork in it, will ya! There's an outlet center in Alpine by the Viejas Casino on the Indian reservation, go get some *THINGS* and do as I say. You want your cut, don't you?"

"Yes," he nearly swallowed the word. "But I don't know what to do up there so far away and when will you call again? You're not deserting me are you? I've done everything you wanted."

"For God's sake, you baby, do as I say and I'll call you tonight. You've trusted me so far, right, so you're just gonna have to trust me now. So get the hell out of town. NOW!" The line went dead.

Jeremy sat for a moment listening to the silence on the phone. He took a deep breath, signaled to the waitress, ordered a house salad, dressing on the side and another diet soda. As soon as it was dark, he left some cash on the table, got up, nodded to his friend at the bar and walked with what he thought was casual dignity out the back door.

❧❧❧❧❧

It had been a long six months. Jeremy Blake bartended at a very private club in Hillcrest. It was the kind of place where closeted gay or bisexual men wanted to go, a place where they could be their true selves and not the image the straight world had of them. Even with all the newest acceptance of LGBT people, there were still men and women who would always be reluctant to admit who they were. And so clubs like this existed. Hidden behind the façade of a simple neighborhood bar, acquisition to the exclusive club upstairs was strictly monitored and expensive. Ironically, the décor appeared not unlike that of an historic gentlemen's club in London. Replete with leather couches, overstuffed wing chairs, dark paneling and heavy drapes that shut out the street below, all–in–all a luxurious place to hide. The club, simply called, "The Club," also boasted several private rooms where secret assignations either casual or serious took place. It was a real coup for Jeremy to get this gig. It paid fairly well but the generous tips—and not only for drinks poured, really helped pay the rent on his dinky studio apartment. He kept telling himself he didn't need much. But when he saw the Rolex watches, the diamond pinky rings and key fobs of deliciously expensive cars the members sported, he began to wonder how he could live like they did. And then *he* came to the club.

Jeremy knew this man wasn't a member. Guests were allowed in on certain nights only. He had to admit: this man was good-looking, so Jeremy put on his best smile as he leaned over the bar provocatively, his tight black tee shirt showed his toned pecs to their best advantage.

"And what can I get or do for you tonight, sir?"

The man grinned at him, "The oldest, best Scotch you have, Sweetie, on the rocks."

Jeremy poured the $100-a-shot Scotch and made sure the man was watching his muscles flex as he scooped the ice into the glass and poured in the smoky amber liquid.

"Here you go, do you want to run a tab?" He thought again, *Good decision to go into debt for the teeth whitening.* He smiled again at the stranger.

As Jeremy put the glass down, the man quickly reached out and put something in his hand. "I've got a question for you. Do you have a minute to listen, or a break coming up soon?"

Jeremy glanced down quickly at the two one-hundred dollar bills the customer slipped into his hand. He looked up at him for a second, turned his head to the other bartender and said, "Going on a quick break, Andy." He pulled open the small gate at the end of the bar and with a quick jerk of his perfectly combed and gelled head signaled the tall and handsome man to follow him. The customer looked at Jeremy with raised eyebrows as he followed him into the room at the back where the liquor and bar mixes were stored. Jeremy shrugged an apology.

"I'm not allowed in the private rooms unless a member gives a written request to the manager, sorry." He closed the door behind them and stepped closer to the other man. He was a little surprised when the man took a step backward, his hands up, palms facing out.

"Whoa, kid, I just need some info and I can surely make it worth your while."

Jeremy folded his arms across his chest. This didn't sound good. "Hey, look, I gotta keep anything about our members on the down low. If I told secrets or gave info, I'd be outta here, so thanks for the nice tip, but I'm going back to work." He put his hand on the knob, but the man reached out and stopped him.

"There's a man who comes here, name of Yano Di Stefano, but he may go by an alias, do you know him?" He spoke in a rush.

"If I do, so what, and who are you? A cop? Now I'm really gone."

"No, really, I can make it easy for you to quit this two-bit gig and live like they do." He tilted his chin towards the door to indicate the clientele on the other side.

Jeremy thought for a moment. His recent rent increase had him digging into his 'fun' account and he owed money to his Vegas bookie for his losing bets on the kick-boxing matches. Not for the first time did he bet on the fighter's body instead of his win-loss record. He took his hand off the door and listened.

And that's how it began. For an extra $200 a week he began an aggressive campaign to win the lust, if not love of one Yano Di Stefano, aka, Sonny D as his fellow club members knew him. It wasn't that difficult, really. Jeremy fit Yano/Sonny's type: muscular, blonde, handsome, alive and willing. The customer told Jeremy to only call him "M" and promised to give him ample help and information to attract and ensnare his prey. Jeremy figured the guy had a James Bond delusionary fixation going on with the secret name thing, but whatever worked. With the information he was given and the draw of a possibly big payout, he smiled and snuggled his way into Yano's life so well that he before long he was settled into a small condo in Mission Hills and given an ample allowance. He even had the occasional use of Yano's bitch of a wife's BMW whenever she jetted out of town on yet another spa vacation. On the other hand, Yano was NOT Jeremy's type. Short, given to soft flab around the middle, extremely hairy and much older. However, Jeremy figured you can't have it all. The relationship was only bearable because of the promise of a wad of money "M" promised when "this little adventure," as he called it, finished.

Jeremy had grown up in a family, if you could call it that, with very little means. Both parents worked at low paying jobs and even though he was an only child, there was never enough money to make him even consider himself spoiled. By early adolescence, he admitted to himself that he was gay. When he tried to explain who he was to his parents, they sadly did what "good God-fearing folk" often did; they kicked him out of the house at 17. That was 12 years ago. He took what little money he'd saved from working at a fast-food job he hated and took the first bus out of his dinky town and headed west. Despite hardly ever having a high-paying job, Jeremy did have good taste and good looks, so he managed along the way. But he was 29 now and tired of just managing; he wanted so much more. Maybe this was his chance at last.

The man "M" had given Jeremy little details as to the "what and why" of the deal. But he kept promising so much money, in fact, that Jeremy asked few questions and despite not liking himself or Yano very much, began to have dreams of living a life of luxury somewhere in the Bahamas, or Caymans or at the very least, La Jolla.

⚜⚜⚜⚜⚜

But now Jeremy sat holed up in a dinky room at the Off Hwy 8 Motel, looking at the cheap clothes and toiletries he'd purchased on the way, hating himself for everything he'd become. Cursing again he tried angrily to get any kind of decent program on the small table-top television. "Dammit! What the hell have I gotten into?" he ranted as he threw himself on the musty bed, and slammed the remote on the floor, watching it as it split open, the batteries rolling out onto the stained carpet.

⚜⚜⚜⚜⚜

Detective Clifford Aloysius Dawson stared into his third class of Red Breast Irish Whiskey.

"See any solutions in there? I hardly ever do, but seein' you're a professional detective and all ..." Declan Neil O'Malley, bartender and owner of The Plough and Stars Pub in South Mission Beach leaned on the polished mahogany bar waiting for an answer. Dawson looked up at the tall Kildare man and frowned.

"No, Dec, no solutions in here, or in the other two glasses." He threw the rest of the deep golden liquid down his throat in one swallow. Declan leaned back, scowling in disapproval.

"That's no way to be drinkin' a fine sippin' whiskey, my man. No matter what your troubles, you gotta treat a good, smooth whiskey like a good smooth woman: nice and gentle.

Dawson shoved the glass over to him. "Well, then get me another so I can treat it better."

Declan snorted, turned and grabbed the bottle and poured a double shot. "It's either a bad case you can't solve or a bad woman you can't get."

Dawson drank his whiskey neat with no ice; the Irish appreciate that. It was one of the things that made Dawson and Declan friends— that, and the fact that they were both great at keeping secrets. There were many sodden nights when the two tough men confided in each other, knowing that

21

whatever they said was not held against them, never judged.

Dawson took a slow, respectful sip of the whiskey. It *was* good, smooth, warm and comforting, like a good woman. Not for the first time Dawson had a brief, wistful thought that the only really good woman in his life was his mother, so might as well enjoy the whiskey. Declan polished a glass, his left eyebrow raised, waiting for an answer. Dawson took another sip, put down the glass and looked up at his friend— his only friend, really.

"It's both, Dec. Goddammit, it's both."

Declan looked hard at his friend, reached for another glass and poured a double shot of Red Breast for himself. He took a sip, leaned down with both elbows on the bar.

"Right, then. I know you can't tell me about the case, but I sure as hell want to hear about the woman."

"No, you don't. Trust me."

"Ach, then its sure'n shit someone I know. C'mon, spill!"

Dawson lowered his head, took a deep breath and blew it out hard. He knew the bartender would not budge until he told him. Resigned and somewhat terrified, he looked up and spoke through clenched teeth.

"Do you remember the woman P.I. who was interfering on the Falco case?"

Declan frowned, then both his eyebrows shot up suddenly, nearly reaching his hairline as he quickly stood up straight. His pale blue eyes fairly sparked in surprise and shock. He opened his mouth to speak but nothing came out. Maureen, the fire-haired assistant bartender stood nearby carefully pulling a pint of Guinness. She glanced over at her boss and snickered.

"Whatever did you do, Dawson? 'Tis surely a bloody miracle; you've stung him speechless."

Declan closed his mouth, grunted and looked over at her. "Mo, mind your pourin' there, you'll make the draught settle badly. And while you're at it, mind you don't sass your boss."

He turned to Dawson and jerked his head to the right. "Come away to the office with me. *Now.* Mo, mind the place for a bit. And make sure you watch old Mick there; he's after glarin' at ya for not refillin' his drink. We'll be in the back."

With that he and Dawson went around the bar and through a door past the pool table. Declan's office had the look and set up for a man who spent a good deal of time there. He called the pub his second home but it was more often than not the only home for this confirmed bachelor. The room had the same dark paneled walls as the pub, with a large desk and two comfortable chairs set facing it. A long leather sofa sat against one wall and a small kitchen against the other. Dawson followed Dec into the room.

"Close the door, will ya?" Declan muttered.

Dawson did as he was bidden then turned to face his friend who promptly smacked him hard upside the head.

"Hey! Ouch! What the hell?"

"What the hell indeed, you great *eejit* of a man! Has the whiskey turned your already feeble brain to porridge? The Salerno wench? Are ye daft entirely?"

Declan turned away in disgust while Dawson shook his head to clear it and tested his jaw to see if it was dislocated. He tried to speak, but thought better of it since his friend still muttered and groused, his voice a low punishing rumble.

"I cannot for the life of me cipher what you're thinkin' or for that matter what you're thinkin' WITH, 'cause for certain it can't be with your head." He turned and tilted his head towards Dawson's crotch. Seeing his friend scowling and reaching for the doorknob, Dec grumbled further. "Aw c'mon then, sit ye down and I'll make you somethin' to eat, ya great miserable fool."

Dawson, still frowning, plopped obediently into one of the worn leather chairs opposite the desk. Declan, cursing under his breath, reached into the mini fridge, took out eggs, butter and cream and proceeded to make two enormous scrambled egg sandwiches. Dawson knew cooking always calmed the big man down so he just sat and waited.

As he piled the eggs onto the dark soda bread he'd made from his own mother's recipe, Declan sighed, "Aw, me Mam was right. An egg sandwich is great with the whiskey. Eat up."

They ate in stony silence for a bit. The warm rich eggs melded perfectly with the solid bread and the melted butter. By the time they were down to the last delicious bites, the two men had mellowed both in body and spirit.

"Thanks, Dec," Dawson mumbled as he picked up both plates and put them in the small sink. The bartender acknowledged the thanks with a slight, not unfriendly grunt. He settled back in his chair, reached for his whiskey and didn't speak until the other man sat down. His voice took on the softer tone of a man gently chiding his errant adolescent son.

"Cliff, tell me, in the name of all that's holy and rational, why her?"

"She just gets to me, Dec. I mean, I know she's an obnoxious, over confident, interfering, *tiring* woman, but still …"

"That she is, and not even Irish to boot. I don't get it. Italian, is she? Well, that's all right. Better that than the mix."

Dawson frowned, "The mix?"

"Irish and Italian, like the one I nearly married." He crossed himself. "A very dangerous woman, that. God never meant them to reproduce, ya know." He reached again for the bottle.

Dawson just shook his head. "Anyway, nothing's going to happen between us for very simple reasons. One, she can't stand me, thinks I'm a fool, two, our professions don't exactly go together that well, three, she made me look like an idiot by bringing in the Falco perp herself while gloating like she'd just won the Super Bowl and four, well there's you know..." His voice trailed off as he self-consciously rubbed his palm over what remained of his once full head of hair and shrugged.

"Ah," Dec said, catching his friend's meaning. He inclined his head as he refilled his friend's glass yet another time. "Well, that's good to hear, if not entirely believable."

"Whaddya mean by that?"

"I mean, Detective Dawson, when you're after something, you're like a daschund heading down the badger hole. You'll fret and fester about this woman like you do your cases, until you conquer or are conquered, m'boy. God help ya, I hope the case you're workin' on takes your mind away from her."

Dawson sat in silence and looked into his whiskey glass, twirling it gently between his two palms. When he not only did not answer nor meet Dec's eyes, the bartender abruptly sat up straight, his desk chair squeaking in protest to the sudden change of position.

"You don't mean she's in the middle of THIS case as well?"

Dawson nodded without raising his head. "See, there's no way to get away from her. She's at it again and right now, I think she may be two steps ahead of me. I tell ya, if she reels in the bad guy before I do again, I'll never make lieutenant, never mind me getting the girl!"

Before Dec could fully take in the import of the policeman's remark, they heard a quick knock on the door. It opened just enough for Maureen to poke her head in, red curls bouncing as she spoke.

"Hey, Dec, there's a woman out here looking for Dawson. Says she knows he comes here after shift and wants to know if he's been about. Should I tell her he's here or not?" She grinned over at Dawson, "She's not half-bad; you may wanna go for it Mr. Cop."

Dawson and Dec looked at each other, shrugged, stood, took a few seconds to steady themselves and followed Maureen out the door. The sandwich had done its work. Dawson felt pretty good despite the fair amount of drink he'd consumed. His head seemed pretty clear, considering. But as soon as he came around the bar and saw her, he gripped its polished edge to keep himself from falling into the nearest stool.

CHAPTER FOUR

"Whoa, looks like I've got a ways to go to catch up with you. I'd better get started." She waved to Maureen and turned back to the stunned Dawson. She patted the stool beside her. "Well don't just stand there, Detective, we've got a lot to talk about." Grinning, she ran a hand through her already messy dark and carefully highlighted hair. "See if you can tell me who said this in what movie: 'This is the way I look when I'm sober. It's enough to make a person drink, wouldn't you say?' " Dumbstruck, Dawson just shook his head.

"Oh, that's right. You suck at the quotes game. Hope you're better at the cop game." Scarlett turned away from Dawson, flashed a smile to the bemused Maureen and said, "I'll have a Campari and soda on ice with a chunk of lime and my friend will continue on the same destructive path he's chosen." Glancing at the gob-smacked Dawson, she tilted her head and continued. "Right, Cliffie, let's get started on making me look better."

"You'll never catch up to the likes of him drinkin' this." Maureen grinned as she set about getting the drinks for Scarlett and the still-speechless Dawson.

"Yeah, well, one of us has to be serious here, ya know. And Campari's good for the digestion, and God knows I'm gonna need a strong stomach to deal with his detective-ness here."

Dawson wanted to gulp down his whiskey, but saw Declan frowning at him from the corner of the bar, so he restrained himself and sipped, holding the warm liquid in his mouth for a few seconds before swallowing. His courage up, he turned to Scarlett and cleared his throat.

"So, what brings you out this late? I mean, it's not a full moon, is it?"

Scarlett snorted a short laugh and nodded her thanks to Maureen before taking a sip of her own drink. "That was nearly good, Clifford. Nah, I heard you were a regular here and needed to have a bit of a chat, that's all."

"Really? About what? Frankly, Scarlett, you never seem to give a damn about talking to me unless you're making fun of me."

"Gosh, you almost made a movie quote there. Careful, I might be rubbing off on you." Scarlett took a longer sip of her Campari and suddenly became serious.

"Look, Cliff, we've got to talk about this Di Stefano case. There's gonna be some really nasty stuff going down and I think, God... I can't believe I'm saying this ..." She shook her head and looked into her glass, then up at him. "I think we're gonna need to help each other on this one, you know, maybe even work together a bit."

Dawson stared at her for a long moment. He felt the glass in his hand about to wobble. He clenched it in his fist and downed the whiskey in one gulp— to hell with Dec. When he could finally speak, his furious low tone surprised them both.

"What the hell is this, Scarlett, some kinda joke? Look, don't even think of jerking me around like this. I'm a goddamned good cop and I don't need your help. Who the hell do you think you are, anyway, Nancy Freakin' Drew?"

Scarlett was stunned, but curious. She sat quietly and let him spew. He slid his empty glass across the bar with a vengeance and continued, leaning in close enough for her to smell the whiskey on his breath and see the small grease spot from his egg sandwich on his blue and white striped tie.

"Listen, Salerno, you screwed me over on the Falco case, remember? That nearly cost me my badge and I'm sure as hell not going to let that happen again. So whatever you think you know better than me, or think you *do* better than me, just forget it, right?" Turning to Maureen, he said loudly, "What do I have to do to get another damned drink, huh?"

"You're done, pal." Dec said quietly but firmly. Dawson looked at him, started to open his mouth to protest, but the big Irishman's scowl and shake of the head silenced him. Maureen quietly placed a glass of club soda with a wedge of lime on the bar near his hand.

Throughout Dawson's diatribe, Scarlett sat silently sipping her Campari through the short red straw. When her glass was empty, Maureen deftly placed a fresh drink in front of her in a smooth, practiced motion, obviously not wanting to miss any of the exchange. Scarlett winked at her in thanks, looked over at the detective and spoke quietly.

"Cliff, are you done, now, because I've got something to tell you and I really don't want to see any more smoke coming out of your little pink ears, all right? It's unattractive." She sat back and waited while he took a drink of the club soda and quietly enjoyed seeing him grimace at the taste before she spoke.

"You've got a mole in your department, Cliff. Somebody knows what went down in the Di Stefano murder and they're on the payroll of his shitty Uncle Cosmo." She held up her hand when he started to speak, silencing him. "And don't ask me how I know, because I can't tell you— privileged info— so you know I can't. And yes, you're a good cop, and no, I don't think I'm Nancy Freakin' Drew, 'cause I'm way better than that sickeningly sweet and clever little bitchlet. Cliff, no matter how rotten this family is, neither one of us wants to see anybody else dead and I know what's left of this pseudo-Mafia bunch can do some real harm. So, do you want to hear me out or not?"

Dawson sat back and looked at her for a long time not speaking. Like a good barkeep, always observant and often intuitive, Declan turned toward them, catching Dawson's attention. The big man nodded and jerked his thumb to the right at a closed-in snug around the back of the bar near his office.

"Come away with ye, now, I've the place for quiet talk."

He kept this snug for important customers or friends who didn't want to be seen in the main part of the pub. He led them to it and as he reached down to open the small half-gate on the high-backed dark booth, Scarlett whistled through her teeth.

"Wow! I'm impressed, barkeep." She went up the one step, slid onto the booth seat and patted the smooth deep green vinyl next to her as she looked up at Dawson. "'Well, sir, here's to plain speaking and clear understanding.'" At his perplexed look, she explained, "Sydney Greenstreet, in the 'Maltese Falcon'. Gosh, Cliffie, were you an underprivileged child or something, never watched any classic movies? Geeze."

"Cut the crap and get to it, will ya? It's already been a long day, and night."

"You're tellin' me! I'm the one with the wrecked car and the sore bod. No sympathy, huh? Okay, let me tell you what I can." They both took a drink and she tried again not to snicker at the face Dawson made at his club soda. The snug was comfortable, but despite the long-ago ban, the high wooden backs of the booth seats still held a slight smell of stale tobacco smoke. Scarlett wrinkled her nose at the scent, but continued.

"I'm a San Diego girl, Cliffie, born and raised. Good city, but every city has its pocket of trouble, you know. It may change with the times, but some things survive, even if very quietly. For a lot of years, there was a Pacific Beach branch of, for want of a better word, the 'family'. Capice?" Dawson just continued to look at her. He didn't nod, move, or even blink. She went on.

"This bunch controlled some of the fishing business not owned by the Portuguese, lots of businesses in P.B., where some of them lived, and import/export stuff as well. All very legit looking, stuff taken care of behind store fronts like restaurants down on Grand Avenue and shoe repair places, some barber shops. Family members brought over from Italy and Sicily to run the legit businesses while the graft and shady stuff went unnoticed. I went to school with a lot of Portuguese fishermen's daughters, so I grew up hearing a lot about the so-called 'dealings'. Always thought it was gossip, ya know, girls' powder room snippy stuff, but there was some truth to the tales. Remember the guy, Basilio Benedetto Calvino? They called him Benny?" Dawson shook his head and smirked, clearly wanting her to get on with it. She took a deep breath and continued, ignoring his attitude.

"Anyway, you should look up the case, at least, educate yourself." *Attitude for attitude, even up,* she thought. 'Several years ago, he supposedly had this great business importing Italian goods and setting up stores, helping some of the guys who might still have places in town. Well, Benny built this huge house in La Jolla, up on the hill. Soledad area, loved the view and thought he was something, being near the big cross. Cost him a freakin' fortune. Real showplace. Only problem, he messed up on his income tax, probably used the infamous two sets of books. You'd think they'd learn, right? So when the IRS came looking, the investigation got too close to some and they got worried." Scarlett stopped to take another drink, ignoring Dawson pretending to yawn.

"So, poor little Benny showed up dead in a gutter in P.B. after having been missing for days. Cause of death: 'undetermined', which, according to my pals at the County Morgue is a 'classification that means the information pointing to one manner of death is no more compelling than one or more other competing manners of death in thorough consideration of all available information'. Mouthful, huh? So detailed I made myself memorize it." Dawson mimed applause, his mouth twisted to one side. "Nice sarcasm there, but I'll take the applause anyway. May I continue, sir?"

Without waiting for an answer, she went on. "All to say, we don't really know how the hell ol' Benny bit it. Body was a soggy mess, case never really solved. His businesses were all in his kids' and wife's names and all the IRS stuff suddenly checked out. His lawyers made all the papers nice and legal and wifey and kids paid a bunch. Lost the house, businesses all got quietly liquidated. Wife wound up working in a friend's dress shop. But everybody else, somehow, quietly taken care of nicely, except for Benny, of course."

Dawson shrugged and pulled at his already loosened shirt collar. "Nice story, but what does this have to do with the Di Stefano case? As you say, all happened a long time ago, and who really knows if there ever was a P.B. Mafia? Just a lot of rumor and conjecture over the years from what I hear. Nothing really criminal stuck to anybody, huh?"

"Cliffie, I know you're not a native here, but believe me, there was a small P.B. 'family' and some are still hanging around loosely, if you know what I mean. Uncle Cosmo is still somehow connected, if that's what it's still called, and he's doing bad things, *very* bad things."

"'Connected', huh? You sound like a bad Scorsese mob movie. Where's your proof, Salerno?"

Scarlett sat back quickly, a look of shock on her face. Recovering, she leaned in close to Dawson, glared at him and snarled. "Before I go on, I need you to know something and never forget it, Cliffie. *There is NO such thing as a bad Scorsese movie, mob or otherwise!!*" She sat back and took a deep breath, ignoring Dawson's scowl.

"Okay, now that that's clear, back to business. As for proof, that's what I can't talk about right now, but I'm close, I really am. Been looking into this bunch for months, and no, I can't tell you why!" She held up her hand to stop his obvious question. "I know Yano was killed for a reason and murder is either for love, lust, money, jealousy, more money and did I mention money? I have a couple of ideas who may have done the deed but I can't nail anybody for sure—yet. What I do know, shall we say, *suspect strongly*, is Cosmo is into something else really foul and maybe you and I can nail him for that kinda Capone-style ya know, get him into that 6x8 stone room without a view any way we can." She stopped for a breath and when Dawson just sat there, she sighed and continued, speaking quickly, hoping to see some sign of interest in the detective's deliberate, blank gaze.

"Yano thought he had a secret life with his little boy twinkie on the side, but he messed up and Cosmo found out and may have figured Yano was too much of a risk. And I admit I have no real evidence of who did Yano in. Now the people who do know what happened are, shall we say, not exactly available. But they do exist and I know it and so, unfortunately, does your mole. It's your mole who's going to mess this case up for you, Cliff. If you and I don't get to him soon or find out how to get to Cosmo, more people may die or disappear. Believe me, Cosmo *can* make people disappear. I can't say any more, but believe me, he already has."

Dawson studied her face. She looked at him directly and didn't flinch. He wiped a hand across his face, his day's growth of beard raspy against his palm. He glanced away for a moment before he spoke, his voice intense. He didn't look up at Scarlett.

"Listen, what you're saying is damned hard to take. I mean, you're saying one of us …," he poked his index finger hard against his chest and repeated, "… one of *us* is dirty." He turned to look at her, waiting. Scarlett's dark green eyes held him. He couldn't have looked away then if he wanted to. Running a hand through her consistently obstinate wavy hair she sighed before she spoke.

"Dawson." Surprise, she hadn't called him Cliff. "Dawson," she said again, her tone soft but clear. "Cosmo is the worst kind of creep there is. My other source has been staking out a residence he owns south from here. Big yellow Victorian with a lot of grounds and a more security than the White House."

Dawson gave a derisive grunt. "Yeah, right. So if it's so damned secure, how do you and your so-called 'source' know all about it? Seriously, who's the source? Another mole in some other place?"

Scarlett took a deep breath and briefly closed her eyes before she answered.

"The house has to be some kinda secret club. Its way out there, top of a hill on a dead-end street. Street is kinda run down and I found out *somebody* is buying up all the other old houses leading up to his. These other houses are far down the street and his is on a big canyon. Comings and goings mostly afternoon to evening, no big loud parties it seems, and lots of big black SUV's bringing people in and out. Tried to talk to remaining homeowners there, the ones that haven't been bought out. No dice. They're either old or 'don't know nothing' or other folks who don't want to say anything, period. The houses that get bought up stay empty for a while and then either get torn down or are rented out to multiple people, so far as we can tell."

Dawson sat back against the dark leather cushion. "So what? You *think* the guy buys up lots of old houses and you know actually nothing of significance about the big one. What *do* you know, Salerno, really? I'm thinking you're just enjoying wasting my time telling spooky stories."

Scarlett looked into her now-empty glass and wished she had another drink. Licking her dry lips she turned to the disheveled detective and met his steady gaze. "I can only say he's dealing in the dirtiest kind of stuff, using people as throwaways and much, much worse. Something really nasty is going on and your mole is in it up to his shifty eyeballs! I know this is rough, but there are some truly innocent people involved here. Yeah, some are just caught up in it by dumb luck and maybe some greed, but hell, they really don't deserve to die, do they? I mean a dirty cop is a terrible thing, but hiding and protecting someone who can do this much harm isn't the right choice, is it?" Another surprise, she reached out and placed her hand on his beefy one as it lay on the shiny resin table top.

Dawson looked down at her hand on his, and she quickly took it away. "Okay, Ms. Not Nancy Freakin Drew, what do you propose we do. How do we work this out together if you can't or *won't* tell me anything?"

Scarlett smiled at him. "Can't tell you all of it *yet*. Meanwhile, I propose, Clifford that you work really, really hard to find your mole. I know you can do that and I promise, I'll feed you whatever info I can find to help you. As for me, well, I'll just need one favor from you, just one." She held up her finger and waited.

"I'm afraid to ask, because I know it's going to cost me somehow, I'm sure of it," he sighed.

"I'm going to say just the same two words Indiana Jones said to Marian: 'Trust me'."

Dawson gave a short bitter laugh and raised his glass to her. "And I'm going to say what he said later on in the same movie: 'I've got a *bad* feeling about this.' "

Scarlett grinned and raised her empty glass to him in acknowledgement.

Declan and Maureen both turned in astonishment at the sound of loud, wicked laughter coming from the snug.

⁂

It was very still outside the bar. A light fog that often crept in from the Pacific Ocean blurred the streetlights and left a slippery sheen on their cars and on the purple blossoms of the Jacaranda trees that lined the streets in this older neighborhood. Unperturbed by the wetness, Scarlett leaned against her rental car, arms folded across her chest as she looked up at Dawson.

"So, you really thought the wife was in the Beemer we were both chasing?"

Dawson, hands shoved deep in his pockets, rocked back and forth on his feet and shook his head. "Nah, with those deeply tinted windows, couldn't be positive. But being her car, we had to pursue, just in case. Why? Do you know who was driving?"

Scarlett gave him a crooked smile. "Cliffie, if I did, do you really think I'd tell you?"

"But you just now agreed to …," Dawson began.

Scarlett straightened up and waved a finger back and forth in front of his face.

"Cliffie, *we* may have agreed to work together on this case, but I'm not raking in a big fat check from the city police department. I'm out here on my own, ya know, and if I don't protect my clients, I don't get paid. So, yeah, some info is just mine and it has to stay that way, for a while anyway."

Dawson sighed and pulled his collar up against the damp. "O.K., I give up for now, Salerno. It's getting too cold and if I stay out here in the fresh air much longer, I may just sober up. How about we talk tomorrow? Wanna meet me somewhere for dinner? It'll give me a chance to snoop around the department for that mole you're so sure is there."

Scarlett pushed a wayward strand of damp hair of her forehead. "God, what this fog does to my hair! By tomorrow you'll be able to cut off a piece and scrub a pot with it." She grinned up at him. "Hey, did you just ask me out on a date? Careful, Cliffie, I either rub off on people or just plain rub them the wrong way."

"I'll take my chances. Besides, we really gotta get on with this case before my chief beats me over the head with it and your mystery client thinks you're not worth your fee."

"Deal. Only one more thing. Did you ever *really* read Nancy Drew?"

"Nah, they were my sister's favorites."

"Sure they were." Scarlett nodded, scrunching up her face in disbelief. Dawson didn't bother to reply.

They agreed to meet at *Ulivo Ristorante* in Ocean Beach at 6:30 the following night. Despite her protestations, Dawson insisted on waiting on the sidewalk until she was safely in her locked car and driving away. He stood for a while looking at her retreating tail lights before he walked to his own car. He shivered as he slid in and closed the door. He punched in the numbers on his cell phone and waited for a long time before the bored voice answered. "Police Department; this is Hooper."

"Hooper, Detective Dawson, badge 165 here. I need a license tail set up."

"Okay, sir, do you want a 24/7?"

"Yeah, on a rental license number T14709, Toyota Corolla, dark blue. But just a tail and surveillance, not for pick up. No perp involved."

The clear sound of typing on the other end stopped. "Sir, if there's no perp or suspicion of crime, I'm not sure this can be authorized."

"What the hell are you talking about, Hooper? *I'm* authorizing it as of *right now!* Did you get that, Hooper? Put it through, or get me your supervisor, what'll it be?"

The typing resumed at record speed. "Got it, sir, it's in place right now. Just tell me where the vehicle was last seen, I'll call a unit on it right now."

Dawson gave Hooper the information, ended the call and drove home. He slept deeply that night, thanks to the whiskey, but his dreams disturbed him. He dreamt he was a contestant on a game show and kept missing every question having to do with movie quotes.

❦❦❦❦❦

✿✿✿✿✿

CHAPTER FIVE

The two voicemail messages on Scarlett's phone were interesting but not as informative as she'd hoped. The first was from her source in the South Bay area.

"Hi, Scar, sorry I didn't get this to you sooner. But all this is from about three days ago. Listen, been able to get inside the big yellow house posing as an SDG&E guy. Dontcha love that I kept all those phony uniforms and badges, now, huh? Anyway, boss man has a smooth operation all right. Big fancy place nice dining room, lounges, the whole magilla. Also, got a sexy lady assistant, Francesca somebody. Legs up to there and all business in a tight skirt. Whoa! Anyway, Filipina worker girl in the kitchen, big Ruskie chef, gorgeous barmaids and security like you wouldn't believe. Big beefy goons everywhere, look like mercenary-type guys. Mean-ass suckers. So, smart lady that you are, your hunch seems to be on the money. I'll send you the photos I took on my phone while nobody paid attention to me. Some layout, Geeze! Let me know if you want me to jump into another disguise and go back in. You know I got a million costumes and I do love to dress up. By the way, is my check in the mail or do we wait *again* for the big pay off? (Laughter) Love workin' with ya, Ms.S. Ciao!"

Scarlett let out a low whistle as she checked her email and looked briefly at the pictures he'd sent. Two pictures caught her eye and she tried to expand both but knew they'd show better on her laptop. She picked it up off of the bed and opened up the email. One she figured was of the young Filipina in the kitchen. The woman was so tiny, her face not visible because her head was bent over her work at the steel prep table. The other was clearer. It was one of the barmaids, a tall auburn-haired young woman. The camera had captured her face as she was picking up a drink order at the bar. Scarlett noticed the shy smile but there was something wary in the woman's eyes and

33

her body language as she stood at the bar seemed to convey tension. Then Scarlett realized her source had shot video of this woman and the lounge. Scarlett let out a low whistle and muttered, "How the hell did you get this? Fella, I have severely underestimated your talents."

The room was just as he said, lush and expensive looking. She watched as the young woman went about her task of delivering her tray of drinks to a table where four well-dressed men were talking and smiling. When the woman placed the drinks before each man, the last man to receive his drink reached out and stroked her arm repeatedly, smiling up at her saying something Scarlett could not make out. Watching the woman in the video put on a forced smile as she tried to casually slip away from the man's touch, Scarlett shuddered involuntarily and rubbed the gooseflesh that had quickly risen on her own arms. *Man! What a lay out is right. Dirty business must be real good, Uncle Cosmo. You are way beyond the definition of creepy!* The next voicemail was a deep voice she knew, speaking nearly in a whisper.

"Okay, so I don't have much. What I do have is that Dawson is in major shit for not getting anything of substance on the Di Stefano murder."

Scarlet shook her head and hit "pause" on the message. "Well no shit, Sherlock! Some help you are."

The message continued. "Been getting sneak looks into the records of nearly every cop in the precinct and can't pin anything on anyone yet. But ..." The voice paused but Scarlett could still hear breathing, so she waited. "Hell, I don't know, just a bad vibe I guess, but I don't want to say anything now. Not 'till I'm more sure, ya know? But, yeah, something's fishy and I'm gonna find out who and what and I'll get back to you. I know you want more and so do I, but it ain't easy, being a snoop, I mean. Not my style. Just damned hard and frustrating. Will be in touch."

"'Not my style', huh? You worthless ...." Tossing the phone on her bed in disgust, Scarlett pulled her smudged navy blue T-shirt over her head, sucking in her breath at the pain in her bruised shoulder. "Ouch! Damn! Wonder what else hurts." She looked down at her jeans and frowned. "Yep, rips in new, expensive jeans. That's painful. Crap." She sat on the bed and took off her shoes, relieved that her back hurt only slightly as she bent over. Standing slowly, just in case, she slipped off her jeans and tossed them and the shirt into her overflowing hamper. "Gotta do some laundry, Scarlett," she mumbled to herself. Sweeping her eyes around her bedroom, she shook her head at the cluttered dresser, the opened, unfinished novel and dirty whiskey glass leaving yet another ring on the nightstand, which she got at a thrift store and hated anyway, the dry cleaning still in its plastic draped over a chair. Muttering on: "And you gotta clean up around here. Rosa would have a fit if she saw this." Another deep sigh, "Truth is, Ms. Salerno, you need a maid, a cook, a person to pick up your dry cleaning, to make an appointment to service your broken car, an assistant to pay your bills on time.

In short, you need a wife! Tough to find for a straight girl like you."

She ran her hands again through her unruly hair, now even more frizzy from the fog. The private cell phone still in her jeans pocket began to buzz. She dug it out and smiled as she listened to the message from her mother. "Hey, *Bella Mia*, all is well here at the *palazzo*. The *principessa* is safe in her bed in the tower and I'm going to my own chamber now. Call me tomorrow, but not until after I've finished watching my stories from today— you interrupted them, you know. But I'll catch up before I record tomorrow's. Sleep tight, *Bella Mia. Ti Voglio Bene.*"

"Ah, Mama, you and your soaps; you're completely addicted! Some things never change," Scarlett said aloud to the now-quiet phone. She yawned broadly and headed for the shower. Pausing to look in the full-length mirror as the water heated up, she sighed, "Dear God, why couldn't you have given me a tall willowy body, but no, got the hips of girl who loves her pasta. Maybe just a bit taller would work and with straight hair? Yep, just like the witch said: 'Snow White lives!'" Seeing that she was being ignored, again, she resolutely laid out her gym clothes and shoes for an early workout; well, maybe not too early. Silently thanking her last client for the funds that allowed her to indulge herself in a whole house music system, she tuned it to the film soundtrack of *Cinema Paradiso* before she stripped completely and stepped into the steaming shower. "O.K., God, I forgive you for the hair and bod because good water pressure and great Italian music is enough of a blessing right now. MMMMM."

Warm, and a little less stiff, she swallowed a baby aspirin, crawled gratefully into bed and was asleep within seconds. Outside, in a dark sedan across the street, two men in cheap suits sat sipping scorched coffee out of cardboard cups. When the lights went out in Scarlett's bedroom, one of them shrugged and spoke.

"O.K., I'll catch some sleep while you watch Missy's house for any action." He pushed his seat back and settled himself.

"Why you first? What's the deal?" The other man was clearly put out.

Without opening his eyes, the first man answered sleepily, "Because, I've got a whole six months seniority on you, and I'm a very big and muscular peace officer."

His partner acquiesced, nodding. "Yep, that works. Sweet dreams."

Just down the block, a black van with deeply tinted windows was parked in front of a bank-owned house. No one had found this suspicious, since it had only been parked there since nightfall. Inside the van two men in very expensive suits sat in comfortable bucket seats, watching small LCD screens attached to the wall of the van.

They'd set up on orders from someone their boss trusted, charged to watch Scarlett's house until further notice. They'd seen Scarlett come out of the house, and drive the rental car out of the driveway and down the street earlier. But since the driveway was long, with the garage at the far end, they didn't see Lizette, her head covered with a black hoodie, come out of the side kitchen door. She'd quickly slipped into the back seat and laid down.

Now, one man turned to the other in the van and spoke as he pulled one of his earphones off.

"Do you want to take a sleep break now, or later?"

"Boss said we shouldn't sleep until the next guys get here."

"Yeah, well that won't be for another six or eight hours, so maybe one of us should."

"You can if you want, but I'm gonna keep watching her house."

"She's asleep by now. What is there to watch?" The first man shrugged and reached for his pack of cigarettes on the shelf next to the small coffee machine.

"Look, you haven't been working for the boss as long as I have, so if it's all the same to you, I'm gonna stay up and watch the monitors and maybe even take a quick walk around the *Strega's* house just to make sure she doesn't slip out the back or through the walls or something."

The younger man laughed. "Yeah, I guess you're right. The boss was pretty pissed when she pulled the vanishing act before. Only one woman drove out and only one came back. Who knows? You think Lizette's in there with the lady dick?"

"If she is, we'll find out sooner or later. And when we do, she'll be sorry she ever snagged his rotten, stupid brother and so will that damned woman detective she hired. The boss'll see to that for sure. He's got plenty of 'interesting' places for them to go. And he'll make sure he makes a profit outta their disappearing act; he always does. So you might as well make some coffee, 'cause we're gonna be here a while."

❀❀❀❀❀

Galina Koshka hated dark rooms. She also hated the cold. The room she was in now was both of these things: dark and cold—just two of the many reasons she left Russia. She wrapped her thin black sweater closer around her body and wished for the hundredth time that she had a cigarette. She closed her eyes and inhaled deeply, trying to somehow magically taste the last smoke she had. *It seemed very long ago*, she thought. *Or was it?* Had she really been in this room so long she'd lost track of time itself? Shivering as she got up from the hard wooden chair that never seemed to warm no matter how long she sat on it, Galina walked over to the dormer window and looked out into the darkness. If she stood on tiptoe and craned her neck to the left, she could just make out the glow of the lights from the deck of her prison three floors below. Her breath quickly fogged the window and all became dark again. "Can you see anating?"

Galina turned toward the voice coming from one of the small cots in the corner. "Not really, Malaya," she sighed. She could see Malaya's small frame shift on the uncomfortable bed. "It iz like Russia: like a forever darkness."

Malaya swung her legs over the edge of the cot, her bare little feet dangling above the wooden floor. "Nothing is forever, Galina, only the love of God is forever. There will be sunshine for us both when we are free again. Remember my name, my friend."

Galina snorted a laugh and had to smile in spite of her own gloom. "Yes, Malaya, I remember vhat your name mean: free and independent. Let us both hope your parents' choice to name you that is happy omen, huh?"

Malaya slipped off the cot and walked over to Galina. She looked up into the light blue eyes that she could see even in the dim light. She put her hands on Galina's tightly folded arms and pulled until she could hold the taller woman's hands in her own. "You must have faith, dear friend. God will never abandon us. We will be free, I know it."

Galina looked down at the small face before her. She stared into Malaya's eyes, almond-shaped like her own, but so dark they reminded her of chocolate kisses. She had come to love this frail little Filipina woman, even though they'd only known each other for a short time. Perhaps their dire circumstances bonded them together but unlike Malaya, Galina had no real faith in God. But she did believe in the cruelty and ruthlessness of their captors. How they each came to be in this frigid attic with its smell of mold and despair was a different story from the one they'd hoped for. But Galina was certain their stories would end the same way and she shivered again, but this time not from the cold.

❧❦❧❦❧

CHAPTER SIX

At first, working as a barmaid in the big yellow mansion had seemed like a dream to Galina. She and her roommate, Malaya had often spoken about how lucky they were to have such good jobs and such a nice place to live. The house they shared with other women who worked with them while not as fancy as the mansion, was so much nicer than either one of them had ever lived in before. Their rent was reasonable, taken out of their wages, so no problem to them. At first. Over the course of the two years they worked there, the rent slowly increased as did their 'insurance' payments. While getting fitted for new uniforms, Galina had asked Francesca, Cosmo's administrative assistant and general manager of the club why and she got the curt reply. "Everything goes up, m'dear. We have bills to pay, too."

Galina always felt intimidated by Francesca, which is exactly what the other woman intended, not only by her officious manner, but even by the way she dressed. This day Francesca was impeccably attired as usual. She wasn't tall, but the four-inch stiletto heels that clicked across the highly polished wooden floor made her appear so. Her dark hair, perpetually shiny and loose, just reached her shoulders. She wore a Chanel Suit, classic black with white piping on the lapels and a snowy satin camisole cut just low enough to be sexy and still tasteful.

Galina swallowed and spoke softly, "Yes, I understand, but I am trying hard to save money for myself, my future, and it is getting harder. And I still have to pay for these new uniforms. When I work café in Russia, I get to keep my tips. Why not here?"

Francesca put a red-tipped index finger under Galina's chin, her sharp acrylic nail biting slightly into the skin as she raised the young woman's face, her dark, cold eyes fixed on Galina's nervous ones. "You need to understand, Galina. We are a very private enterprise, so we take care of the accounting here, and we divide the tips according to our rules. And by now you know you are to follow the rules of this club exactly? It is VERY important that you understand. Do you?" Her gaze was so deep and steady, Galina stood rigidly, afraid she'd shiver and show the manager just how uneasy she was. She gulped and began to nod, but the fingernail point was still in place, so she just said, "Yes, Mz. I understand. I vill work hard, you vill zee."

Francesca gave her something that should have passed for a smile. "Good!" She removed her finger, turned and spoke to Darcy, the blonde cocktail lounge manager, "Make sure she has the new lace tights only under that skirt, and don't forget, no bras. We know the members want that 'natural' look about our girls." She and Darcy shared conspiratorial half-smiles, half-smirks. As she walked out of the fitting room, she picked up a tissue out of the box on the fabric cutting table and vigorously wiped her finger.

Back in her office, Francesca picked up her phone and left a message for her boss, Cosmo. "Sir, the Russian girl is complaining and questioning again. Think we should keep an eye on her and possibly the roommate as well. Tell Leo and the other drivers to be alert. May have a runner here." Francesca was right, as usual. That's why Cosmo had her as his right hand. Her instincts were always spot on. She'd saved him a lot of grief and money over the years and that made her indispensable to him and they both knew it. She was that good.

Galina's fears grew more and more as she watched one woman after another simply disappear from their house without any explanation. A few days later she confided to Malaya she had seen people in Russia disappear the same way and was going to find a way to escape. Hearing this, Malaya had crossed herself and shivered.

Galina asked, "What is it?"

Malaya leaned in and spoke quietly. "I thought women only going on to get a better job, like they always talk about. But my roommate before you come, Sarah, one day she just gone. I come home from late shift, closet door open, drawers open, all her things gone, like she left in hurry, some things dropped on the floor. Sarah very neat, never toss things around. I ask other women here, they say maybe she got better job, but when I ask Goren the chef, he say stop asking questions; not my business."

Galina nodded solemnly. "Yes, we must make a plan, and very soon."

A week before Lizette Di Stefano hired Scarlett to spy on her husband — the ill-fated Yano— Galina and Malaya were forced to make a plan to run away and set in motion the events that would bring the two women and Scarlett together in strange and dangerous circumstances.

❈❈❈

CHAPTER SEVEN

It started one late night when the young Russian woman couldn't sleep. Galina was smoking a cigarette in the dark in the bathroom she shared with Malaya and three other housemates. Pondering for the hundredth time how she could get away from this place, this employment she now saw as a prison, she drew deeply on her cigarette, shivering as she thought of the ugly man who had, not for the first time, run his hand up her short skirt that night. He had pulled her close and grasped her buttock, squeezing hard. When she flinched and instinctively pulled away, the trouble began. "What the hell! Who do you think you are, princess?" He reached out and grabbed her wrist, pulling her down so close to his face, she could smell his breath reeking of Scotch, garlic and something akin to death as he fairly spat at her. "I pay damned good money to be treated well in this place, so you better make sure I AM treated *really well*. Get it? Me and your boss go way back, bitch, so I can make it easy for you or very hard." He leered at her frightened look. "And speaking of hard..." As he pulled her hand towards his crotch, Jackson, like the good bouncer he was, appeared seemingly out of nowhere.

"Hey, there, Mr. G. How we doin' here, everything all right?" He said this as he released the man's grip on Galina so quickly the ugly man looked down at his empty paw as if he'd suddenly lost something. Jackson turned just as swiftly to Galina. "Go to the break room, I'll meet you there. Go now!" Turning back to the now protesting customer, Jackson, ever professional, slipped into the plush seat next to him. "Mr. G. our apologies, sir. She's a Ruskie, right off the boat and still learnin' what's up, if you catch my drift." He gave the petulant man a conspiratorial wink. "Trust me, I'll take care of this, and her. How about I send over Lorraine there? She knows the ropes around here and is a real pleaser. And your drinks are on the house tonight. Okay? Need some food or anything, huh? We can get you a room for the night if you don't wanna drive. We know you're good for it. Been with us a long time, huh?"

Mr. G. pouted for a few minutes, looked over Jackson's shoulder at Lorraine, petite, blonde, great figure, and relented. "Sure, Jackson, no trouble from me." Leaning in he asked, "Lorraine, she like to travel? Got a good friend in Colombia who'd love a picture of her. Maybe take a little trip? I've helped your boss before. Whaddya think? Maybe work a deal? If it works out, maybe good for all concerned, huh?" He gave a guttural laugh. Jackson simply smiled.

"We'll see, Mr. G. Let me send Lorraine over. Let's see how it goes and me, you and the boss maybe can talk." Standing and patting the now perspiring man on the shoulder, Jackson walked over to the smiling Lorraine and pulled her toward the bar, leaning down to speak quietly in her ear.

Standing in the dark bathroom, remembering, Galina sighed as she took one last drag, lifted the toilet seat and tossed the butt inside. Watching it sizzle and go out, she was just about to flush when she heard a noise of tires crunching on the driveway outside, but, oddly, saw no headlights. Closing the lid on the toilet, she knelt on it and pulled herself up to look out the narrow open window. The black SUV was instantly recognizable as one of the many always around the big yellow house. Two men got out, one carried a black bag that looked like a doctor's bag, the other, clearly in charge, was mumbling to the second man. Galina could not make out what was being said, but ducked down quickly as the men approached the house. She warily crept down and went to the bathroom door. Cracking it open a fraction, she strained to hear. The front door was opened, a bit of light shown through a slightly opened door down the hallway. She instantly knew the light came from Lorraine's room. The little blonde was so friendly and always very certain bigger and better things were ahead for her. The man who seemed to be in charge Galina recognized as Leo, and he went purposefully down to Lorraine's room. Without knocking, he and the other driver walked quickly into the room and he closed the door behind him. Galina held her breath and waited. She heard voices: his, Lorraine's, but the small woman's voice soon rose in pitch and was quickly silenced. She heard what sounded like someone bouncing on a bed. Then: silence.

Within minutes, Leo came out of the room, an unconscious Lorraine tossed over his large shoulder like a rag doll. The other driver entered the room quickly, unfurling large garbage bags. Galina pulled back into the black security of her hiding place, letting out the breath she hadn't realized she was holding. Shortly, she heard more movement from the room, and dared to peek out. The dark figure of the driver passed her carrying the now-full garbage bags. As he slipped by her, he dropped one of the laden bags, cursing quietly as he bent to pick it up not noticing that he left something on the floor. Galina heard the engine of the SUV start up and within a few short minutes they coasted down the driveway and were gone quickly, the household undisturbed as if they'd never been there at all.

Galina waited a few minutes, her breath coming out in shallow spurts. She could feel her heart pounding against her ribs. When she was sure the taillights of the car had long disappeared, she ventured out into the darkened hallway towards hers and Malaya's room. Feeling her way along the wall, she crept slowly, grateful most of her housemates were working the late shift at the yellow house. As she went past Lorraine's room towards her own, her bare foot caught something on the floor. She bent down to disengage what had stopped her. Pulling it off her foot she held up a red thong panty, the very one Lorraine had held in the laundry room the day before, twirling it around her finger, waving at Galina in goodbye.

And so their careful planning began. But as the poet said, "the best laid plans …" In the attic now, Galina opened her eyes, scrubbed the tears from her cheeks. But she couldn't stop re-living the rest of her journey, the journey that started out so hopefully and had led to this place, her imprisonment and the terror of what might lie ahead. It all played out like a bad movie projected onto the dark window in front of her.

❀❀❀❀❀

Five days before Scarlett met Dawson at the bar and after weeks of planning, Malaya and Galina made their escape. They planned a shopping trip so they would have the one driver who wasn't the brightest of the fleet. Usually the drivers wouldn't even let the girls go to dressing rooms at the same time, let alone the rest room, but this driver, Tony, seemed a bit more sympathetic and Galina knew if she said she had "girl stuff" to do in the rest room, he'd relent quickly. And so once in the grocery store late in the afternoon, as the sunlight began to fade they went through the big doors behind the dairy case, past the restroom and out into the alleyway. They ran down the darkening alley to the street, and kept running until they got to a small boutique in the row of restored Victorian shops near the trolley stop in National City proper. The saleswoman was a bit surprised that they each found something so quickly, but smiled as they took the merchandise into the dressing room area. Changing quickly into the different clothes they'd packed, they pulled their baseball hats down low on their foreheads and quickly left the shop. It was fully dark now, and some street lights were turning on, but the two women looked around, saw no one in pursuit, and ran towards the trolley station. When they got to the station, they stayed in the darkness and waited. Breathless, Malaya whispered, "Remember, if somehow we get policeman talking to us or asking questions, we tell him, take us to police station and we tell them all about the big house, *Si?*"

Galina nodded, shivering despite the balmy night. She turned to Malaya and asked quietly, "If we get to Los Angeles, can ve get to Hollyvood from da stazion?" She was so nervous, her studiously practiced English gave way and her Russian accent slipped back.

"Maybe by a bus, I think, but we must keep moving, Galina, we have to get to my cousin's to be safe." Safe. It was what they both longed to be.

"Well girls, maybe not Hollywood just yet, huh?" Galina gasped as she recognized the voice. It was the main bouncer, Billy. He and Leo had come up behind them in the darkness. Before they could move or speak, Billy made sure they saw the glint of his switchblade as he and Leo grabbed each woman by the arm.

"Now, *ladies*," Billy's voice was low and gruff, "let's not make a noise, a scene, nothin', you hear, and that way we can make our way back to the house without anybody getting, shall we say, scratched up, huh?" Galina tried to pull away, but quickly felt the point of the blade poke into her upper arm, drawing blood. Billy tightened his grip and spoke with a low growl into her ear.

"Listen, bitch, I have no problem cutting you and your little friend here. The boss don't care as long as I don't leave a visible scar; his customers may not like that, so don't tempt me. Come on, nice and slow."

With that, he and Leo propelled them out of the waiting area to the two black SUV's waiting on the street. Billy roughly pushed Galina into the back seat where another bouncer was waiting. He grabbed her and shoved her down on the floor as the two cars took off. Whenever she tried to move, the bouncer put his big foot on the back of her neck, forcing her to lay still, tears running down her cheeks onto the rough carpet. She feared Malaya was suffering the same way and dreaded what might happen next.

Once stopped, the two women were dragged into the back entryway of the big yellow house, pushed into the service elevator and then propelled into Cosmo Di Stefano's office where he, Francesca, and Tony were waiting. Malaya reached for Galina's hand as they stood before the big desk, trembling. Billy pushed them apart, crossed his beefy arms across his chest and stood between them, glaring at one then the other.

Cosmo sat puffing on his big noxious cigar for a few minutes before turning to Tony. "Come here, kid," he said around the cigar. Tony approached the desk, hands behind his back, head bowed as he waited for Cosmo to speak.

"You know you fucked up, right? These two, you were supposed to watch, you know they nearly got away, huh? You have any idea what would happen to our whole operation if they talked to the cops, you stupid little shit?"

Tony opened his mouth to speak, but snapped it shut when he saw the look on his boss's face. He just put his head down again and nodded. Cosmo paused for effect before he took the cigar out of his mouth and spoke again. "If Billy here hadn't given me the heads-up that you were slackin', I'd never have known, and we'd all be in it deep! So that's why I sent him to trail you and these two bitches, 'cause he figured you weren't up to the job of keeping tabs. And he was right, wasn't he, *idiota?*" Again, Tony nodded, silent and pale.

Cosmo continued, his voice deep but frightening, "So now what do we do, huh? Tony, you got a plum job here, but you blew it. I figure I gotta put you someplace else, 'cause you can't cut it here."

At this, Tony found his tongue. "Boss, no, I promise I'll be better, this won't ever happen again, I swear. I don't wanna go nowhere, please."

"*Stai zitto!* Shut it! You will go where I wantcha, and no crap, *capito?*" Turning to Francesca, he continued, "So now, what plans do we have for these two, huh?"

Sighing, Francesca looked the two women up and down. "Well, Boss, I figure we can make suitable arrangements for both. The little one we can ship off to the client in Argentina who likes the little Asian types. The Russian would work out well for the client in Dubai, don't you think? He likes her type. I'll send their files out tonight, but we can't keep them here. Too risky. Mountain house for the time being, okay?"

"Yeah, that'll have to do." Cosmo turned again to the hapless Tony. "And now for you, punk. Billy, you and Leo make sure Tony here's got enough warm clothes so he can enjoy his time on outside guard duty at the mountain house for now; then we'll figure out someplace else to ship him, *if* he can manage not to screw up again. You and Francesca got this, 'cause I'm done." He reached for the whiskey decanter on the desk and poured himself a large drink, clearly dismissing them all.

"Sure, Boss," Billy said, and grabbed Tony by the collar and propelled him out the door. Leo touched his fingers to his forehead in salute to Cosmo and followed the two men out. Francesca pushed a button on the desk and three more men came in with handcuffs and black hoods. She gestured towards the two shivering women.

When Galina saw the men, she screamed, "No!" and tried to run out of the room. One man grabbed her, and she heard Malaya scream as she backed away from the other man. He quickly grabbed the little woman, threw her on the floor and put his knee into her back. She struggled as he pulled her hands back, handcuffed her and then slapped her hard as she twisted around, trying to wriggle away from him. Galina kicked out at the man who held her. She was taller and stronger than Malaya, and scratched his face trying to knee him as he pushed to pin her against the wall. She spat in his face. He cursed and punched her in the jaw. Stunned, she went limp and he threw her to the ground, pinned her down and cuffed her, roughly grabbing her by the hair, yanking her head back painfully as he put the hood over her head. Cosmo stood at his desk chuckling with glee at the scene playing out before him.

"Ha, this is like a good Tarantino movie scene! Get 'em guys, but don't damage the merchandise."

Once the women were both immobile on the floor, Francesca came over with a syringe for each. She methodically injected each woman in the neck, and they went limp in seconds. Shaking her head, she tossed the spent syringes in the fireplace and watched as they popped and melted. Turning around, she saw the two men hoist the women over their shoulders and leave the room. Taking a small flask of hand sanitizer out of her pocket, she cleaned her hands and said to Cosmo, "Well, that's a shame, really. Two good workers to replace, but I'm pretty sure we'll get a good price for them both, Boss, just trust me."

"Don't I always, Frannie Baby?" Cosmo handed her the drink he'd poured for her and they raised their glasses and drank to yet another successful business transaction.

Francesca tossed down her drink and set her glass on the desk. She turned and walked towards the door with a well-practiced sway of her hips, knowing her employer liked to watch her walk away. Just before she opened the door, she turned, flicking her silky dark hair over her ear. "But you know, Boss, you really have to quit smoking those horrible cigars. Not sexy, not sexy at all." She gave him a quick wink and left as the sound of Cosmo's deep laugh followed her out the door.

⁂

Now, remembering their capture and rubbing her sore jaw, Galina leaned her head on the cold window of the attic room and watched as her breath clouded the glass. Behind her came the soft murmurs of prayers from Malaya, prayers Galina sadly believed were in vain.

Below the mountain house, the fog of the previous night had burned off to reveal another beautiful San Diego day. Another day that would bring an unlikely group of people together: a determined private investigator, a struggling police detective and two women fearing for their lives.

⁂

CHAPTER EIGHT

In the city below, the fog from the night before lifted nicely, revealing a bright morning sky. But a deeper fog lingered brutally that same morning in the mind of one hapless San Diego police detective.

After four large cups of black coffee, plus two super-sized Red Bull drinks, twenty soda crackers, three aspirin and ten antacid tablets, Detective Clifford Dawson's eyes could finally focus on the computer screen in front of him. Was it only a few hours ago he was arguing with Scarlett in the bar? God, he wanted more sleep! The foam ear plugs he had saved from his last airplane trip helped dull the sound of horribly loud conversations, the infernal clacking keyboards, and the harsh noise of the clodding footsteps of the other detectives in the squad room. He just couldn't understand why these seemingly intelligent, thoughtful peace officers had to be so decidedly unpeaceful. Hunched over his desk, he surreptitiously held a cold, comforting can of diet soda against his pounding temple. He had been staring at the familiar face on the screen for a long time. Using his right hand to work the mouse, he kept the makeshift cold compress on his head while he scrolled down the screen and focused on the information there. Just as he thought, Scarlett had done everything by the book. An honors graduate in college; major: criminology, with a minor in psychology, then law school. She worked for two years at a prominent law firm in the city before obtaining her private detective license. No official problems with the police force were listed. At this Dawson laughed aloud and then regretted it at once as he gritted his teeth against the pain it caused.

"And what's so amusing this fine morning, detective?"

When Dawson didn't respond, the tall, very blonde detective at his shoulder reached over and pulled out one of the ear plugs.

"Hey!" Dawson whirled around as the other ear plug was yanked out, this time by a very hefty, very black detective. The partners, Toby Monroe, often called Marilyn because of his wavy blonde hair, and Jamal O'Sullivan, referred to as Black Irish because of his mixed parentage, stood side by side, perfect opposites, grinning down at the pale, disheveled Dawson. "Rough night, Dawson, or just a normal one for you?" O'Sullivan's dark eyes danced at his own quip.

"Oh, snap!" Monroe replied with the accompanying swishing gesture; his hair wasn't the only reason the rest of the squad called him Marilyn. They fist bumped each other and laughed.

"Guess you two don't have anything to do. Got all the streets of San Diego safe all by your widdo selves, did ya?" Dawson growled at them.

"Actually, we came by to give you your best news of the day. Whatcha lookin' at? Something fun?" Monroe said, as he bent over Dawson's shoulder to look at the computer screen. Monroe was as quick as he was nosy. Dawson, as well as many others on the squad, found him consistently annoying. Before Dawson could move or complain, Monroe snatched up the mouse and with a quick slide, Scarlett's face was once again on the screen.

"Oh, lookie Jamal, the detective has a pretty suspect."

"Get away, Marilyn." Dawson pushed Monroe's hand away and reduced the screen but not before O'Sullivan had taken a quick look.

"Hey, she's not bad. Anyone we know, what's she up for. She a hooker?"

Dawson turned on the two of them and snarled. Neither his head nor his stomach was in the mood for their wisecracking. "She's not a suspect, perp or hooker, you salt-and-pepper morons. Now if you don't mind, what's this best news business? Some of us do work around here ya know."

"Well, let's not get our panties in a bunch, shall we?" Monroe remarked as he straightened his already perfectly knotted iridescent blue tie.

"The captain wants to see you. *if* you're still working on the Di Stefano case, that is. Hard to tell when the murder's been nearly a week old. Jamal and I should have been put on this, if you ask me."

"Well, nobody did so thanks for the news, it's not a week old, so now run along you two and play cops and useless like you always do." He stood and ran his hands over his wispy hair. Reaching into his desk drawer, he grubbed around until he found a mint leftover from a Chinese restaurant. He quickly unwrapped it and popped it into his mouth as he pushed past the two of them, pointedly ignoring O'Sullivan's last words.

"Touchy, touchy, Dawson. No need to kill the messenger here. Let's go, Monroe." With a quick glance at the departing detective, O'Sullivan patted his partner on the shoulder and walked away.

Halfway to the Captain's office, Dawson reached in his pocket for his notebook. Cursing himself for having a still muddled head, he went back to his desk. He snatched up the notebook and shoved it in his shirt pocket and hurried down the hall, hoping this meeting wouldn't last long.

Captain Maximillian Guadalupe Ortega Chang was living proof that San Diego has long been known as one of the top-ten most cosmopolitan cities in the United States. With a Mexican mother, a Chinese father and a Chaldean wife from Iraq, one could say their family holiday parties were, at the very least, interesting. With his ethnicity it was a minor miracle that he had made the height requirement for the department. He excelled in the Police Academy, though, graduating at the top of his class. No affirmative-action strings needed to be pulled to put him on the fast track to promotions. Before he made captain, he completed a master's degree in forensic criminology in just eighteen months. He was known as a very thorough, organized man who had no qualms about annoying the County Coroner as well as any and all CSI teams with his knowledge of forensics and his complete hate for disorder. Dawson knocked on the open office door, and saw Chang once again reading the Di Stefano file. The captain's bright yellow highlighter squeaked loudly as he made another determined, perfectly aligned mark on the page before him.

"Yeah, come in! Close the damned door." His slightly high-pitched voice always made Dawson shudder.

"You want to see me, Cap?"

Chang put the top on his highlighter with a purposeful snap and motioned Dawson to the wooden chair in front of his impeccably ordered desk.

"Going over the Di Stefano case. Nasty stuff. Somebody really wanted him gone."

"Yes, sir, they did." Dawson nodded, not enjoying Chang's grasp of the obvious.

"Any leads, detective? Would be really nice to hear you have some." His voice edged a little higher, but there was no mistaking his seriousness.

"Workin' on some good ones, Cap. Got some outside help with this one."

Chang sat forward in his chair at Dawson's last words, making the detective instantly regret he'd uttered them.

"*Outside* help? What the hell does that mean, Dawson? Don't tell me you're working with some petty snitch again. Do I have to remind you about the last time? Or have you already forgotten why you don't have a partner right now?"

"No, sir, you don't have to remind me."

"Yeah, maybe I do. You lost your last partner because of a lousy snitch. And you know where your ex-partner is now, huh?"

Dawson hung his head, wondering again why Chang could just not let go of this past incident. "Yes, sir, I know. Believe me, he made a great partner and I wish things turned out different, but how could I know?"

"You were his partner! How can you tell me you *never* knew the snitch was his cousin and to save his own skin he revealed what your partner was—

is??" Agitated still, Chang began to stumble over his words and quickly got control. Everyone in the department knew control meant everything to Chang, and yet he remained as tough a cop as any Dawson knew. In fact, he had seen the captain reduce very burly men to shaky little boys in a heartbeat.

Spreading his hands palms up and trying once again in vain to ease away from the irritating topic, Dawson spoke quietly, "Look, Cap, this all went down a long time ago, and we both know Jesse is in a much better place now."

Chang glared at Dawson. "Yeah, if being the headliner at the nightclub 'LIPS' on El Cajon Boulevard is a better place, I guess so. Only it's 'Jessica' now, I hear. God! Such a good cop, too. Damn it, Dawson."

The uncomfortable detective spoke quickly to change the subject. "Cap, I'm working with a P.I. now, a good one, and she's got some good info on the Di Stefano family that I know will help us out. We're really close on this one, just need a bit more time."

"Close? How close? Any leads on the wife, the shitty brother? I'd like *anything*! And I'd like it yesterday. Do you read me, detective? *Yesterday*! And this P.I., a *she*? God!" He clamped his jaw shut with a snap that made Dawson wince.

"Sir, please trust me; what's going down here is not pretty…"

"IT'S NEVER PRETTY, DAWSON, IT'S A FRIGGIN' MURDER! I DON'T CARE ABOUT PRETTY! I WANT A SUSPECT AND I WANT ONE NOW!"

Chang's office had glass all on one side. Dawson could see heads raise and look towards the glass that vibrated with Chang's outburst.

"Sir, I'm gonna promise you we'll get this done. You gotta trust me on this. I know this P.I.. She's completely legit." He again held up his hands, palms toward the captain as if to ward off another tirade. Chang took a deep breath. His face went blank, an expression Dawson knew meant that his boss was practicing some internal kind of Tai Chi, to relax his innards. When Chang finally spoke, his kept his voice low and his words measured.

"All right, detective. Tell me about this *woman* P.I. and why I should trust either one of you with this case. Please make your statements brief and choose your words carefully. You are very close to being taken off this case. The department can't… *I* can't *and* won't have another fiasco resembling the Falco debacle. I've got other detectives just chomping at the bit to get this case, so for God's sake and yours, give me reasons not to." With that, Captain Chang sat back, interlaced his fingers, stretched them across his chest, placed his elbows on the arms of his chair and waited.

Dawson knew a hot seat when he sat on it. He took a great deep breath, took out his notebook, frowned a bit when he saw a page missing, but flipped the previous pages and started at the beginning. He told Chang all he knew about Scarlett, her background, the accident, her meeting with him and why he wanted to work with her, but not her name nor that she was the PI who gave the mitigating information that revealed the crooked judge on the Falco case. He told him what little he knew or suspected about Cosmo's 'extra' dirty little business ventures. He told him everything about the case, everything except about the suspected mole in the department. He didn't tell him because he wanted to catch that bastard all on his own.

❧❦❧❦❧

CHAPTER NINE

Scarlett didn't date. That didn't mean she was a Vestal Virgin or anything of the sort. She had dates for her high school proms. There was one semi-serious boyfriend in college, and a quite serious, if somewhat one-sided relationship with an associate lawyer at *Griswald, Lacey, Rabinowitz and Matsua*. But that ended when the associate realized that, one: she was serious about being a private investigator, and, two: resented mightily that she was so much smarter than him. He did get over both of these obstacles sufficiently enough to remain not just her friend, but to be her legal counsel many, many times. It didn't hurt that he had a relative in the police department who proved to be very helpful to Scarlett whenever she needed inside information. Proof that there were good moles and bad moles— it just depended on which side of the garden they dug.

So now she sat in her favorite booth at Ulivo Restaurant. She smiled as Jackie, the tall waitress she knew so well, came over to her.

"Hey, Ms. Scarlett, you're lookin' mighty fine tonight. Big doin's?"

"Nah, Jackie, you know me. No real dates for this busy girl. Just waiting for an acquaintance. It's all business."

"If you say so." Jackie set a glass of the fine house Chianti in front of Scarlett as the young Hispanic bus boy approached the table.

"Your to-go is ready, Ms... Where did you say it should go?" He held the stay-warm pizza carrier in front of him.

Scarlett handed him a folded slip of paper and a tip. "Just open this when you get outside, don't ask or answer any questions from anybody and scurry on back here when you're done, Jorge. *Muchas Gracias!*"

Jorge looked at the folded paper, then the currency and grinned widely. "*De nada, Senorita!*" Jackie's eyes followed Jorge as he dashed outside into the warm twilight.

"So you're sending food out, but actually eating in?" She turned to Scarlett, one perfectly-penciled eyebrow arched.

"Just a funny thing I do now and then, Jacks, you know me, whimsical to the end."

"Yeah, right, whimsical like a Mack Truck! I'll come back when your 'acquaintance' gets here."

Dawson arrived ten minutes late. He stomped into the doorway, turned his head quickly from side to side, his eyes took in all of the intimate room before lighting on Scarlett. Frowning, he made his way around the center tables and slid into the booth opposite her.

"I don't like my back to the window," he spat out, without saying hello. Scarlett's smile of greeting vanished quickly, as she sat up straight and surveyed his rumpled appearance. She'd worn a deep claret-hued knit dress with a low V-neck that met all her fashion criteria: it was simple and comfortable. Her make-up was subtle and carefully applied to bring out what she thought was her best feature, her eyes. Even her often wild and wavy hair was fairly tamed. Her only concession to making herself looking somewhat dressed up was the gold and diamond heart pendant her father had given her for her eighteenth birthday, and the Italian gold hoop earrings she'd purchased for herself from a charming old gold dealer on the Ponte Vecchio while on a solo trip to Florence. She'd even splashed on a little floral perfume, so she was pretty taken aback by Dawson's lack of grooming.

She didn't expect much, but really! His sparse hair stood up in springy coils. He sported a once- dark-brown, now fading, pitifully rumpled suit. Added to this non-sartorial garment was an extremely ugly orange and red tie which was loosened and had crookedly slipped down his open-collared, pale-gold shiny polyester shirt. To top off this sorry ensemble, he looked bloody angry as he reached for his full water glass and downed the liquid in two swallows. He eyed Scarlett's wine like a man who'd spent the night in the desert. She waved to Jackie and turned to him, speaking quietly.

"So, Cliffie, who peed in your Cheerios this morning?" He opened his mouth to speak, but snapped it shut as Jackie approached.

"Jacks, get my friend here a glass of your lovely Chianti, won'tcha?" Jackie's ready smile faded when she saw Dawson's dark visage. "You want I should bring a half-carafe, or maybe a full carafe?"

Scarlett saw Dawson's nearly imperceptible nod and ordered the full carafe. When the waitress had departed with a knowing wink, Scarlett turned to Cliff and spread her hands as if to say: "What?"

Dawson glared at her, head down, eyes tilted up. Their normal hazel color now almost orange and looking like they could shoot white sparks at any moment. He leaned in towards her and his words came out through clenched teeth.

"First, my captain ground out a new one for me this morning. Second..." He took a deep breath and sat back slightly as Jackie brought the Chianti. When she attempted to pour it for him, he put his hand on top of his glass and without looking at her snarled, "Just leave it." Scarlett nodded to the startled Jackie, who turned quickly and left, her long braid twitching angrily across her straight back.

Dawson gripped the carafe so hard his knuckles turned white as he poured himself a full glass. He drank greedily, making Scarlett cringe at the sight of him chugging this very smooth, eminently sip-able wine.

"And second ...," she prompted warily.

His glass came down on the table with a muffled thud and he reached again for the carafe as he growled. "Second, you sent A PIZZA OUT TO MY STAKEOUT TEAM?"

Scarlett's eyes opened wide with feigned innocence. "Well, yeah, Cliffie, I figured they'd be hungry since they'd been shadowing me on all my little errands today. And it *is* the all-meat special. Wrong choice? Is one of them a vegetarian?"

He took a deep breath, and while the vivid crimson of his face paled into a lighter pink, he still looked like he was about to explode. "How long have you known about the tail?"

She opened her menu and casually looked over the choices. "Spotted them first thing this morning when I walked by my front windows wearing my very tiny nightie. "Hope they enjoyed the view. We should order, I'm starved and everything here is so good." She reached for her wine and gave him a lightly triumphant smile.

He sat silently for a few seconds, then gave up and grabbed his menu. Still looking very angry he gave up and closed the menu. "Tell you what, since you always know everything anyway, how 'bout you order for me?"

"Really, you trust me to do that?" Scarlett grinned. "Well, Okie-dokie!" She signaled Jackie and ordered the linguini with white clam sauce for herself, the spaghetti with mushroom sauce with a side of sausage and meat balls for him, and extra garlic bread twists for both.

He calmed down considerably over the salad. The three glasses of wine certainly helped. Reaching for a second twist of the fragrant, warm, heavily oiled-and-cheesed bread he finally spoke.

"So, if you are so good at knowing who's tailing you, how come you don't know exactly who this mole in the department is?"

"First, I don't claim to be magical, Cliff, and second, spotting a tail is, well, 'elementary' dear Dawson. It's one of the first things you learn in Private Investigator School."

Cliff gave a derisive snort. "There is no P.I. school and last I looked you didn't go to the police academy."

"Okay. So let's just say its women's intuition. Does that make you happy? Now, can we talk about the case, please? What have we learned today, Cliffie?"

He ignored her pre-school teacher tone and waited to respond while Jackie and Jorge placed their steaming plates before them. For just a moment he was lost in the marvelous aromas of garlic, rosemary, basil and crushed red pepper emanating from the comforting food. He shook his head, reached for the grated Parmesan cheese and began.

"Well, my captain wants me to have a suspect before him yesterday. And did I mention that he is *not*, repeat *not* happy that you and I are working this case together? However, he does *not* know who you are and our past, shall we say, history, specifically the Falco debacle. *And,* I still don't have any leads on the mole. *And* I sure as hell didn't tell him about that!"

"Hmm," Scarlett said quietly, "'What makes life so difficult? People?' "

Dawson glared at her, not even bothering to ask what movie that quote came from and stabbed his fork into his plate. The sauce that spattered his clothing did nothing to improve his considerably less-than-stylish appearance.

Scarlett expertly twirled the linguine around her fork and winced as she watched Dawson cut his spaghetti with a knife and fork. She lowered her eyes briefly and enjoyed a rich bite before she spoke.

"Chang shouldn't be angry we're working together, because we're not, you know. There's your first mistake. *I'm* working this case and *letting* you know what I know because I'm pretty sure neither one of us want to see any more dead bodies lying around. Now, do you want to know what I've learned and what I've *decided* to tell you or should we just enjoy our meal and say 'night'?"

"Okay, Okay, spill," he said, around a mouthful of juicy fennel-herbed sausage.

"I know that the mole in the department has been inside for a while, and he's been on the payroll of Uncle Cosmo. I suspect there is drug peddling and or usage involved along with some other nasty stuff. And believe me, Cosmo's into the nastiest stuff around. But whether Cosmo has something on this cop or not, he sure as hell owns him now." She took a large drink of wine before continuing with some apparent difficulty. Dawson ate and waited.

"How's your food? Good, huh?" She stalled and was sure he knew it.

"Yeah, it's really good. How do you know this place?"

"My mom lives nearby and, being Italian, you know, we can all cook pretty well, so we're pretty picky about Italian restaurants. This one makes the cut."

"Nice. Doesn't your mom live up on Santa Monica Avenue?"

Scarlett's eyes widened. "How do you know that?"

Dawson smiled and pointed to his chest with his fork. "Hi. Detective here."

Scarlett smirked at him. "Cliff, do you know why donkeys don't go to school?" He shook his head.

"'Cause nobody likes a smartie-ass! Now how much more do you know about my family, my life?" She put her fork down and waited.

Dawson told her all he knew about her: her sister the nurse, married to the doctor, where they worked, where they lived, that they were loaded with student debt. He knew about her late father coming from Sicily and working as a landscape gardener for the city. He praised Giuseppe Salerno's advancement to landscape designer by hard work and study. He even knew about her father's legacy of beautiful gardens still thriving in Balboa Park. She admitted she was impressed.

"O.K. Dawson, lots of that is public record, so I can't give you that much credit for top sleuthing yet. Tell me something that'll shock me."

Dawson grinned. "Your mom, Rosa, seems to go through care givers like shit through a goose. Her neighbors report she's had several. She must be a tough one. Like mother like daughter, right? Are you two that much alike?"

"Well, as my Irish friend says, 'they don't lick it off the grass', so yeah, I guess I've inherited a lot of her toughness." She felt anxious; he was getting too close. She needed to get him off this track. She couldn't tell him everything just yet.

"So, who else knows all about me? Did you happen to share these tasty tidbits of knowledge with anyone else?" She held her breath.

"Well, I don't think so." His voice was casual. "I did the checking myself and I don't have a partner at the moment, so I dig around on my own."

Scarlett pushed her plate away, her food half-finished. "Look, Dawson, I'd really appreciate it if you'd leave my family out of this, especially my mom. She's old and, well, doesn't always approve of my, um, chosen profession."

Dawson sat back, sipped his wine, and smiled. "Gee, I can't figure why. I mean, one daughter goes to a prestigious college and gets her RN, then gets her certificate, or whatever, in neo-natal intensive care, works at one of the best hospitals in the city, marries a handsome, brilliant doctor. The other daughter finishes law school but chooses to become a private dick and muck around in other people's dirt. Now why wouldn't a mother be equally approving and proud?"

"I didn't say she wasn't proud, just that she wished I'd done something different. Do you know the old Italian joke about the three women talking about their daughters?" She didn't wait for a reply— she desperately wanted him to forget about her mother and the so-called caregivers.

"So these three old Italian ladies are sitting crocheting, and you know when there's three of anything, somebody's gonna be an odd one out. First lady says to second lady: 'Cara Mia, I saw your daughter the other day. What a lovely girl, so clean and modest and always so kind. She'll attract a fine husband, I know.' Second lady says to first lady: '*Grazie, Cara Amica,* she is a good girl. By the way, I saw your daughter at Mass the other morning and it wasn't even Sunday. So faithful, so virtuous, some man will be lucky to have her for a wife.' They both turn to the third lady and can't resist. First one says: 'So, I saw *your* daughter the other day, walking the street with two men. She seemed very happy, laughing and smiling in her bright, low-cut dress.' Second lady: 'Oh yes and the men were constantly taking turns kissing and hugging her, and then they went into the inn together. Such a lively girl and *so* popular.' They waited for an answer. Third lady looks right at them and says: 'Yes, she is a popular girl, and men do like her, but I'm proud of her all the same. Do you know why?' They shake their heads and she replies: '*Finche non fume!*'"

Dawson frowned, shook his head and shrugged.

"'*Finche non fume!*' It means roughly, 'but she doesn't smoke'. That's the big deal. An Italian girl can do lots of stuff, even act like a *puttana* as *long as she doesn't smoke!*" Scarlett spread her hands wide, palms up. "See, that's why my mom may not totally approve of what I do for a living, but she's sooo happy I don't smoke that it all evens out."

Dawson gave her a slight smile and while she knew he really didn't understand, she hoped she'd distracted him from the subject of her mother. She excused herself to go to the ladies' room. While there, she checked the burner cell phone. One message from Rosa; only, it wasn't her voice; a deep male voice replaced the warmth of the wine and food in her stomach with a five-pound block of ice.

"Well, so this is the famous lady dick, Salerno. Your mama is a real nice lady. Too bad she keeps such bad company. How about we take them both for a little ride? We'll be in touch, Salerno. Somebody who knows you told us to tell ya, 'don't call us, we'll call you.'"

CHAPTER TEN

Dawson looked over the dessert menu as he sipped the last of the Chianti. Before he could make up his mind between the tiramisu and the chocolate lava cake, Scarlett grabbed the menu out of his hand. Bending low, her face close to his, she muttered in a hoarse whisper, "Pay the bill and meet me outside right away!"

"What?"

"Just expense it, or whatever, but move, *now!*"

Stunned, he watched her rush out of the restaurant. She gave a stiff smile and slight wave to Jackie. He fumbled for his credit card, cursing her under his breath. When he finally got outside, she was pacing back and forth on the sidewalk, her high heels coming down with such force he thought the cement would crack beneath them.

"What the hell, Scarlett ...," he began, but she cut him off. She came close to him and gripped the lapel of his shoddy suit jacket.

"Listen, Dawson, and don't interrupt, damn it! Those shitheads of Cosmo's have my mother! You've got to get in your car and follow me up Santa Monica Avenue and *now!*"

He opened his mouth to ask how she knew, but she had spun around and was running down the boulevard towards her car. He just made it into his sedan as she sped by him, pulled an illegal turn, ran the red light and tore away from him. Dawson cursed her again, reached out, put his magnetic police light on the roof, and squealed after her.

At the top of the steep hill, Scarlett screeched to a halt in Rosa's driveway, and flung open her door, leaving the car running, gun in her hand. Her headlight signal wasn't answered; she knew her mother wasn't there. Dawson was right behind her, pulling his gun out of his shoulder holster as he saw hers.

"A Glock? Jesus, Salerno," he muttered, briefly stunned but impressed by her choice of superior firearm. He crept forward as she waved him to her side on the porch. She spoke in low whisper, the slight quaver in her voice betraying her anxiety.

"Cliff, I'm gonna go in. The door's open. Rosa would never leave it unlocked. Keep close."

He touched her shoulder. "Mind telling me what the hell is going on before I risk my life, Salerno?"

She whirled on him, eyes flashing, her mouth a feral snarl. "*Not Now!* Just follow me. Shit!" She turned towards the house bent slightly, kicked off her shoes and turned to push the front door open wider. Dawson clicked the safety off his gun and stayed close behind. The house wasn't dark. The drapes were drawn shut as they always were, but there were lights on in the living room, dining room and kitchen. Guns held two-handed in front of them, the unlikely pair walked slowly into the living room, their eyes and weapons sweeping from side to side. Scarlett stopped and called out to her mother. No answer. She jerked her head towards the hallway and waved Dawson on into the kitchen. Out of habit, he called out "Clear" each time he found a room empty. Within a few short minutes they each determined the house and the back yard were empty.

Scarlett came into the kitchen, eyes wide and searching. "There's food on the counter; the dishes aren't cleared. She'd never leave it like this. They've got them and they left in a hurry."

"Them?" Dawson frowned. "Who else was here?" She didn't answer. He grabbed her arm roughly. "Scarlett, who else was here, who else did they take? What the hell is going on?"

Scarlett took a deep breath and closed her eyes. Opening them and focusing on Dawson, she spoke in a flat, dead voice.

"I was hiding Lizette Di Stefano here with my mother. Mom helps me protect my clients sometimes. Kinda."

Dawson was speechless. He stared in disbelief at her for a long moment. Suddenly her words came in a torrent.

"Yano hired me to watch his wacko boyfriend, 'cause he was sure he was cheating on him. That's who you saw in the Beemer. Lizette hired me to prove Yano was cheating on *her*, 'cause that would violate their pre-nup and she'd get a great settlement and so I took them both on. I thought it'd be an adventure, ya know … ."

"But Yano got himself murdered, and you figured you'd protect the wife and find the murderer all by yourself, and get a big load of cash, but now what, huh, Salerno? Now what?"

Scarlett wiped the sweat from her upper lip. "Slow down, will ya? I have to think, I have to figure out where they took them."

"How the hell do you propose to do that? You've really …"

But she wasn't listening. She'd hurried into the living room. She was at the television cabinet turning the large statue of the Virgin Mary around. Exhaling in exasperation, Dawson reached for his cell phone.

"I'm gonna call for back up and a forensic team. We gotta find something."

"Yeah, you do that," Scarlett answered him absently, as he gave orders in clipped tones to his precinct officer. "Got it! Rosa, you rock!" Scarlett pulled the small camcorder out of the backside of the statue. "Cliffie, we've got video. We can figure out where they've gone!"

Dawson ended his call and frowned at her. "What?" She ignored him for a few minutes, which only irritated him more. He did another quick walk-through the house, mumbling to himself until Scarlett's excited voice drew him back into the living room.

"I installed this 'nanny cam' in the statue, see. So if there was ever a problem, Mom could activate it and we'd have video of what happened. See?" She held up the tiny camera with a trembling hand. The sound of sirens screaming up the hill towards the house nearly drowned out Scarlett's explanation.

"Mom always records her soaps, so I made this really simple. The statue's next to the old video recorder. All she had to do was push the globe at the Blessed Mother's foot, see? And the lens is in the rose bouquet she's holding and a mini-CD in Mary's tummy. Piece of cake! Do you have a computer in your cop car?" She quickly opened up the statue and removed the small disk.

The backup officers were shouting at the open front door. Dawson yelled "All clear," and the room suddenly filled with men in tan uniforms holding lots of guns. Scarlett ignored the cop talk and the stomping around and grabbed Dawson's arm. He winced at the strength of her grip.

"Cliffie, DO YOU HAVE A FRIGGIN' COMPUTER IN YOUR CRAPPY COP CAR?"

"Yeah, yeah, let go, will ya!"
She kept the solid hold on his arm and yanked him towards the front door as one officer tried to talk to him.

"I'll brief you later. Been a kidnapping, old lady, young woman, check the house for evidence or signs of struggle. I'll be back … ." His voice trailed off as she propelled him towards his car. Minutes later, the shaky images on the computer screen showed Scarlett and Dawson a scene she'd never wanted to see.

"Wait, just let me pause my stories." Rosa's voice was strong and steady, just a little higher pitched than usual. Scarlett's heart jumped as she saw the pink floral pattern of her mother's blouse grow smaller as Rosa walked away from the camera. Two men stood in the living room, semi-automatic weapons in their beefy hands. Dawson swore under his breath. A third man's deep voice was heard. He seemed to be speaking to Lizette but neither was visible. Scarlett recognized his voice as the one who'd left the voice mail.

"So now, *Mrs. Di Stefano,*" the emphasis on her name clearly was in no way respectful. "How about you and your little friend here come along with us? Uncle Cosmo would like you to pay him a visit."

Lizette's shaky response came next. "Okay, yeah, but leave her here. She's got nothing to do with me, really. I just rented a room from her, ya know, to hide out for a while. Leave her alone, right?"

The unseen man gave a short laugh. "Don't think so. Matter of fact, we know who's on the other end of this cell phone. Right, old lady? Yeah, I think we'll just leave a nice message for your daughter and then you can come along with us."

Rosa piped up, loud enough for her voice to carry. "I'm perfectly happy staying right here, young man! I assure you I have no intention of going with you. Now if you'll get on with your business, I have dishes to do." She walked over to the television cabinet again. "Now, did I remember to pause this thing? "Scarlett gasped as she realized what her mother was doing. Rosa's hand appeared in close-up for just a second as she quickly moved the statue. The men stayed occupied with Lizette, who could be heard shouting and cursing at them. They shouted back, trying to drown her out. In the middle of this ruckus, none of them noticed Rosa moving the camera-laden Virgin statue around so the third man was now visible.

"Shit!" Dawson exclaimed, putting his head closer to the screen. "You know who that is?"

"Can you roll it back?" Scarlett crowded in to see better.

Dawson pushed the cursor over the screen and froze the frame. "Yeah, it's the uncle's main man. His name is Luca Annunciato Trentino. We've been trying to get something on him for a long time. Figure he's the one who killed the judge in the Falco case."

"You mean the crooked judge who wound up on the take in that case?"
Dawson growled, "Yeah."

"Too bad you guys didn't find that out before he got iced."

His hoarse grunt was the only reply. The reminder that Scarlett had cracked that case still stung.

They started the video again and saw Lizette, still protesting, but to no avail. Rosa at her side now, trying to calm her down.

"Now, Sweetie, let's just do what they say before one of them gets foolish." She turned to the large man and spoke loudly. "Now where we're going; will it be cold? Because you know, I'm an older lady, very susceptible to the cold, so I'll need to know if I need my big coat."

There was a guttural laugh. "Lady, if you'll just shut up! Yeah, you should have a coat. God, one of you goons go with her and make sure she gets her coat, hat, gloves whatever the hell she needs. You, glamour girl, come with me, get your coat, too, I guess. Jesus! What a pain you women are. No makeup, no fancy stuff, just get going!"

Rosa's voice again from outside camera range, "Oh, is it far? Is that why you're in such a hurry? I hate really long drives, you know. Give me a headache, they do. Oh, and I do hope there won't be lots of twisty roads, just hate to be carsick."

"Well, you might just have to tough it out, Grandma. Just get your damned coat and shut the hell up, will ya?" One of the men could be seen hustling toward Rosa's voice. He stood close by her while got her coat out of the hall closet and slowly put it on. Luca roughly grabbed Lizette and put plasti-cuffs on her wrists. Once Rosa had her coat on, he cuffed her as well.

Scarlett gasped again, "Oh, God! Oh Rosa, you are something else. Do you know what she just did, Cliff?"

Dawson continued to look at the computer screen. Watching the men pushing Lizette and Rosa towards the front door, he shook his head in answer to Scarlett's question.

"She's trying to let us know she's got a clue as to where they're taking them. Cliff, Mama and I know from my sources and Lizzie that Uncle Cosmo has a place in the mountains by Cuyamaca Lake! I told you he's into bad stuff. That's where he hides his most precious cargo." Dawson started to ask what she meant, but she continued in a rush.

"Wait, what the hell is she doing now?"

They watched as Scarlett's mother once again began to cross the room towards the T.V. and the statue. One of the men reached for her, but she moved too fast.

"Gotta make sure my stories get recorded again. Never can remember if I did that," Rosa mumbled. But as she got to the television the man grabbed her arm. She turned on him and despite the plasti-cuffs, deftly pinched hard the hand that held her. He yelped.

"Now, you just keep your hands to yourself, young man!"

He pulled away stunned, rubbing the welt on the back of his hand. Luca growled at him from the end of the room.

"Frankie, grab her and come on! It's getting late."

"Yeah, I'm comin'. Now, listen lady, you gotta come with me, and now." Frankie's tone was more pleading than ordering. Rosa had clearly intimidated him. He turned to Luca and said lamely, "Boss, I can't just grab her, she's too much like my Nonna!"

"Get her now, or your Nonna will have one less grandson, *tu capisci?*" Luca moved one step closer to the two of them. Frankie looked at Rosa and tried to grab her again. She pulled away.

"All right, all right, just let me find my rosary beads, they're here by the Madonna somewhere." She turned to the statue bent slightly pretending to look around the top of the cabinet and mumbled in Italian softly. *"Andiamo a montagna, Bella Mia."*

Aloud to Frankie she said, "Oh, here are my beads, right where I left them. O.K. hot shot, let's go." With a wink and a blown kiss to the Madonna, Rosa turned, took the bewildered Frankie's arm as if they were off to Sunday Mass and walked out her front door.

CHAPTER ELEVEN

Scarlett disconnected the USB cord, grabbed the mini CD. "Back this thing out, Cliffie," she said as she slid out of the car.

"What?"

She tossed the CD in her still-running car and headed up to the house. Dawson hurried to catch up to her.

"Scarlett, what the hell?" He tried to grab her arm, but she shook him off.

"Back your car out, so I can move mine, dammit!" She pushed her way past a uniformed officer and opened the entryway closet. Reaching in, she pulled a battered gym bag out and opened it up. Dawson reached into Scarlett's car turned it off and pulled the keys out of the ignition.

"What are you doing?" Dawson demanded, following her into the house.

"Can't go chasing around the mountains in a dress, gotta find … good!" She pulled out a pair of scuffed athletic shoes, faded black jeans, a long sleeved shirt and a jacket.

"You're not going anywhere, Salerno. Kidnapping is matter for the police and the feds. You're done here!"

Scarlett whirled on him. The look in her eyes made the officer watching take a step back. Dawson stood firm.

"Look, Dawson, this is not any kidnapping junket for you and your little friends here. This is my case *and my mother*! You'd feel the same way if you'd ever had a mother, which I'm beginning to doubt. Now, like it or not, I'm going up there! So move your car. I gotta change." She tried to push past him towards the bathroom but he grabbed her arm and held fast.

"Cuff her," he said to the stunned officer.

"What the hell?" Scarlett turned to kick him as she struggled to get away.

"I mean it, Salerno!" Dawson expertly dodged her kick and spun her around, pinning her to the wall. Scarlett's breath whooshed out as her cheek hit the cool pale green plaster.

"I'll cuff you and take you to the station if you don't calm down right now and let me do my damned job." Scarlett had momentarily stopped struggling but he didn't relax his grip. The officer took out his handcuffs and waited. Dawson's voice softened only slightly as he leaned in and spoke in Scarlett's ear.

"Listen, I promise we'll do all we can to get her back safely, but you gotta chill a little. Let me call this in, get the sheriff and feds involved and we'll move on this right away. Don't make me get any rougher. O.K.?"

Scarlett turned her head as best she could with Dawson's thick hand holding her by the back of her neck.

"Sure, Cliffie, that all sounds good except for one thing: I know where the house at the lake is and you don't! The title for the house isn't in Cosmo's name, but I know it's his. I got better sources than you and your lame crew at HQ. So getting them to try and find out will just be a big waste of time. We don't have that kinda time and you know it. So you can either follow me or we go together; your call, Hot Stuff."

Dawson flinched and stared at her in disbelief. After several tense seconds, he emitted a growl low in his chest. Waving away the handcuffs and the bewildered uniformed officer, he slowly let his grip on her ease.

"Shit! All right, I'll call this in, and you go change, but you're riding *with* me, not ahead of me. He held up her car keys for emphasis. Got it?" He let her go and she whirled on him with a triumphant sneer.

"Two birds, one stone, Cliffie. You call it in while I change in the back of your car. Saves time. Let's go." She grabbed the gym bag and her shoes, ducked under his arm and went out the door before he could turn around. Dawson quickly gave cursory instructions to the officers and the forensics team to lock down the house when they were finished. He knew deep down he was taking a risk not calling in the FBI right away, but figured there was always time. Besides, the Fibbies always horned in on the good cases, anyway. He shook his head and muttered to himself, "Yeah, more time to get into more deep shit. What the hell."

He found Scarlett in the back seat talking on her phone as he slid into the driver's seat. He put his own phone down when he heard her speaking.

"Rinder, hey, still got your big-ass dog squad? Great! Got something fun for you and the pups."

Dawson whirled around, frowning at her. She gestured to him to start the car and continued talking. "Yeah, it's the big stone house you and me staked out on the sneak a while back. The one on the north side of the lake; nothing around it for acres. Yep, that's the one my source told us about and your team's been watching. Great idea of yours to keep it unofficial so far. Security gates in front will be closed—probably electronic with a generator back up, so cutting the power won't work. And we know they have their own dogs, so you and your guys gotta be careful. Sure, I'm on my way with an … associate." She ignored another fierce look from Dawson and went back to her call.

"Yeah, but we will need all the deputies you got on this one. SDPD guys can't take this down. They'll be back up. We gotta move fast before somebody calls in the Fibbies. Okay, meet me at the lake store and we'll go up from there. Remember what we talked about before; could be some really bad collateral damage here, so let's make this work. Be on your phone." She put the phone down and turned to Dawson.

"Why the hell are you so slow getting out of here? 8 East to Hwy 79 and pronto, Cliffie. And don't use your rear view mirror to watch me change. They only do that in movies and I should know. Now move!"

"Who the hell did you call, Scarlett?" Dawson snarled.

"A friend of mine in the sheriff's department. He's gathering the cavalry and we can meet up. Now can you please get us the hell out of here? Time's a wastin'!" She pulled the dress over her head and Dawson quickly turned away.

"Salerno, *I* was calling the sheriff." His hands shook as he pushed the key in the ignition, trying to put the vision of her black lace bra out of his head.

"Yeah, but you didn't and I have an 'in' with this guy, so we're covered." Her voice sounded muffled as she put the black tee shirt over her head and bent to pull on the jeans. Dawson cursed under his breath and stomped his foot on the accelerator. Scarlett fell forward against the front seat as he squealed out of the driveway.

"Shit, Cliffie, one car accident a month is my limit. Try to get us there in one piece, will ya?" Red light on the roof whirling, siren shrieking, they sped and bounced down the steep hill, took the right turn onto the unusually quiet Sunset Cliffs Boulevard on two wheels. By the time Scarlett zipped up her jeans, tied her shoes and put what she figured were helpful "instruments" in her socks and pockets, they were on HWY 8 East.

The chatter on the police radio picked up. Scarlett leaned toward the front seat, straining to listen to the conversation between the dispatcher and the other officers.

"Badge 846, request for back up acknowledged. All units east notified." The dispatcher's voice crackled over the radio.

Dawson responded curtly, "846 proceeding on 8 East. Advise number of units available."

A deep voice responded over the unit open to both the sheriff and police frequency. "10-4 SDPD 846, Deputy 770, of sheriff's canine unit en route and standing by. Got four of my best guys and dogs ready. Hey there, 846, got my buddy Ms. Scarlett with you? You lucky man, you! Whoo Hoo, fun times ahead tonight!"

Sounding almost relieved, Scarlett said, "That's my boy, Rinder! Hear that, Cliffie, we're covered! Just like Sherlock and Watson—'The game's afoot!' Drive steady, I'm comin' up." She threw her left leg over the seat and climbed into the passenger seat.

The Highway Patrol responded to the call from Rinder. "Hey, has Salerno got a lead on the *capo*? We want in. Can we play?" Dawson slapped Scarlett's hand as she reached for his hand-held two way radio.

"God, Scarlett, is there anybody in law enforcement you don't know or haven't talked to about this case?"

"Head of the Secret Service doesn't return my calls, but other than that… Hey, at least 10-4 my CHP guys, we could use them if Uncle Cosmo decides to take off."

Dawson grumbled a response to the officer and then asked for radio silence until they got to HWY 79. Scarlett stuck her tongue out at him and checked her gun. She put the extra clip in her jacket pocket, checked the safety. While she made a pretense of sitting quietly, her body language conveyed her tension. Dawson glanced over at her and took note. Her arms were crossed so tightly around her body that her fingers were white. She'd popped a large piece of bubble gum in her mouth and was alternately chewing furiously or blowing huge bubbles and popping them, with a loud, strawberry-scented snap. After a few minutes of this, Dawson reached over tentatively and let his hand hover just above her knee.

"We're gonna get her back, Scarlett. We'll get the bastards, and your mama will be fine." He heard his words and knew instantly how lame, how very policeman-reassuring-clap-trap they sounded, and quickly put his hand back on the steering wheel. Not for the first time, her response stunned him into silence.

"Forest Gump said it right, Cliffie. 'Stupid is as stupid does' and I'm afraid I've been real stupid. Real, real stupid. I should have told you earlier what I know about Uncle Cosmo." Something in Scarlett's quiet, regretful tone hit Dawson hard. He felt his stomach tighten, but said nothing and waited for her to go on.

"My friend Rinder and some other friends in a special investigation division confirmed to me what Lizette told me when this job started with her, a while back. It was also confirmed by my other source and, no, I can't tell you who it is. This was before Yano bought it, and his unfortunate demise gave Lizette more reason to get lost, you know." She paused and Dawson just nodded silent encouragement, afraid to speak lest she not continue.

"You know about the Human Trafficking Task Force that the governor appointed some time ago? Well, at first, the group reviewing and investigating started studying what info they got from Vice and Sex Crimes. But there is so much more to this than sex crimes or even sex slavery. Human trafficking is in everything, Cliff. These people are your busboys and girls, waiters, house cleaners, farm workers, shop workers. They come from loads of other countries besides Mexico; more than you would think come from our good old USA. So many runaways, so many broke kids who are lured with promises of drugs, good money, or a so-called glamorous life. Estimates read more than 300,000 victims now, and growing faster than stats can be accurately gathered. It's seriously sick, Dawson, and Uncle Cosmo is in it as deep as any *capo* can be, and, from what we figure, has been for a long time. We just gotta get him and kill his whole sick business once and for all."

Dawson let out the breath he hadn't realized he was holding. "Scarlett, you know how big this is? We've been trying to find at least one of the heads of this racket in our area for a long time. Just hard to get funding for education of officers, prosecutors, you know the excuses as well as I do. SDPD has suspected Cosmo of lots of crap, but haven't had luck pinning this on his sorry ass. He must be hiding this operation behind the drug and other stuff he's running. Lately it's been like 'maybe we can Capone him' you know, get him with IRS violations, but, shit, *this* is what we want. We want to put him and his bunch of thugs away forever! God! I wish you'd clued me in sooner, before he ..." Dawson stopped, not wanting to put voice to what they were both thinking.

"Yeah, I know, before he snatched my mama. Now he's taking her to where Rinder and my buddies figure he's got more victims hidden. One of my sources even sent me video he got at the big yellow house I told you about. Some of these people look so scared and lost, ya know? Mostly young, pretty women there, doing all kinds of work if you get my drift. Can you go faster, please?" She bit her lip and turned her face quickly to stare out the window. The last lights of Alpine were behind them and her pulse quickened as they turned on Japatul Road, went under the bridge and sped down Hwy 79, climbing farther into the dark, dark mountains.

CHAPTER TWELVE

The north hill facing Lake Cuyamaca commands the best view of the lake, the meadows, and wooded areas that rim the glassy water. There are few houses on this hill, fewer since the last big fire. Some of the residents just gave up after the firestorm flattened their dream homes for the second time. "Property for Sale" signs dot the hillside. Some hearty souls set up trailers or motor homes with the thought that they could at least move a home on wheels if fire threatened again.

People who chose to live in this area, an hour's drive from San Diego and only nine miles from the old historic mining town of Julian, want to be remote for many reasons. The beauty of the vast Cuyamaca Rancho State Park is legendary to hikers, backpackers, lake fishermen, and tourists from all over the United States. As a peaceful oasis between the "big city" and the often tourist-crowded Julian, it calls to those who wish to be in the quiet of the back country and yet close enough whenever the need to be in a more cosmopolitan area beckons. At more than half the land still wilderness, the homes in the area will always be few and far between, just the way the residents liked it, for reasons as different and diverse as the residents themselves.

Cosmo Dante Di Stefano was a mean man, but he was also a practical man. Like the wise little pig in the story, Cosmo built his house of stone. Not only did he build his huge house out of stone and block, he put in superior water and well systems. His electronic security devices were designed to convert to generator power in the event of fire or if the high winds of summer knocked out his electricity.

The entire ten-acre property was so secure, that the sheriff deputies assigned to the area called Cosmo's lake home the "Fortress Fagioli". Like all fortresses, this one held secrets inside: safes behind portraits or panels, rooms that held small arsenals, and the always-useful hidden, locked attic rooms.

Inside his fortress tonight, Cosmo Di Stefano stood looking out the huge living room window at the dark lake across the road. His eyes surveyed the terraced property below. Although he could not see them in the darkness, he was confident his men and guard dogs were walking the perimeter, armed with their dimmed flashlights and night vision goggles. Cosmo eschewed the large floodlights his far neighbors often installed on their home and garages. He liked his home, like his life, to be in the shadows as much as possible. Taking a long drag on his twisted, rope-like imported Italian cigar, he enjoyed the strong smell of the smoke as it fogged up the window. A very definite voice behind him caused Cosmo to hunch his shoulders up towards his large ears.

"You know, young man, that cigar is most annoying and besides being harmful to *your* health, the second hand smoke is not good for the rest of us."

Rosa sat primly in a chair so large her feet dangled inches above the dark inlaid bamboo floor. "And is it too much to ask to have one of these rude men get a footstool for me? I'm not that comfortable in this huge chair, and with these things on my wrists, I can't get one for myself." She held up her hands with their plasticuffs binding her slender wrists.

Cosmo turned from the window and gave a quick nod to Frankie who rushed to the other end of the long room, snatched up a small leather ottoman, and placed it in front of Rosa's chair. He adjusted the stool as she placed her feet on it and beamed as she purred a sweet, "Thank you."

"O.K., Frankie, that's enough sucking up to the *Strega Nonna* here. Go make yourself useful someplace else, if you can. Geeze, kids!" Cosmo waved Frankie away, took another sip of his Black Sambuca and bent to stub out his cigar. He straightened and spread his hands, palms up, towards Rosa.

"Better now, Mrs. Salerno? Comfortable?"

"Oh, yes, thank you, much better. Now if you'll just take me home ..."

Cosmo's smile was more of a sneer. He turned to Lizette, whose small frame was nearly swallowed up by the red leather sofa. She sat wide-eyed, also bound, repeatedly rubbing her wrists and began trembling as Cosmo spoke to her, his voice harsh with sarcasm.

"Well, my dear niece, why don't you tell your little keeper here why we can't take her home, huh? You got her into this mess, you little bitch, now the only way out of it is to make you both disappear. So go ahead, explain away. Me, I'm gonna go get another drink, 'cause I don't want to be in the same room with you three right now." He drained his glass and shot a fierce look at the other terrified person on the sofa. He left them with Luca on guard, sitting in the chair across from them, his beefy hand making the semi-automatic he held across his lap look like a toy. The tense tabloid remained frozen until an approaching voice made the three prisoners look up.

"Hey, Luca, m' bro, you keeping everybody all snug and tight in here?"

The young man with the carefully highlighted blonde hair leapt to his feet when the owner of the voice appeared from the hallway.

"You bastard! You set me up!" Jeremy shouted, as he propelled himself towards the other man, shaking his tightly bound fists. His trajectory was halted suddenly by the black muzzle of Luca's gun shoved sharply into his chest.

"Don't even think about it, baby fag," Luca snarled.

Lizette let out a little yelp and pulled her feet up and buried her face in her knees. Rosa leaned forward, fascinated by the action, her hands gripping her rosary beads.

Jeremy scowled and lowered his balled-up fists as he backed away from Luca. Harsh, high-pitched laughter came from the newest member of the group.

"Ha! Sit yourself back down, you little fool. You know it's a wise man who knows when he's outnumbered and outsmarted, but then again, you're not known for your wisdom are you, Sugar?" With that, Detective Toby Monroe walked up to Yano's boyfriend, Jeremy Blake, punched him hard in the stomach, and watched with delight, as the younger man folded in on himself with a grunt, and fell to the floor.

Rosa shoved the ottoman to the side with strength and agility belying her age and size. She pushed herself out of the deep chair, shouting at Monroe, "That was a rotten thing to do! *Animale!*"

Taken by surprise at how quickly she came towards him, Monroe let out a shriek of pain as Rosa reached both hands up and whipped him across the face with her rosary beads.

⁂⁂⁂⁂⁂

In the parking lot of the Lake Cuyamaca store, Deputy Sergeant Travis Wayne Rinder greeted Scarlett warmly despite the crisp chill in the air. "Long time no see, no fun, Ms. Scarlett!"

Rinder, who seldom went by his given name, had been with the San Diego County Sheriff's office since he graduated college in his early 20's. Having worked his way up by diligence and with strong penchant for studying the criminal mind, he rose quickly in the ranks of the department. In this way, he and Dawson were similar, in other ways, not so much. Not a nerdy bookworm by any means, Rinder was a man who, as he often said, "liked to work hard and liked to play harder." And therein laid the major difference between him and the SDPD detective: Dawson really didn't know how to play, hard or otherwise. Dawson fit more of the soft-bodied, nose-to-the-grindstone profile than Rinder did.

An athlete in high school, Rinder worked out these days at his local crossit gym, having always found the challenge of competing with himself more fun than competing with others. His family always had dogs, big dogs.

Consequently, he grew up also loving to train and enjoy the companionship of animals he often thought were better company than humans. Being the deputy in charge of the canine unit was a dream job for him, and he relished the cooperative mix of men and their beloved and trusted four-footed partners. Indeed, when one of his dogs was up for 'retirement', it was not unusual for the animal to spend his last days as a family pet for Rinder, his extremely patient wife and their sons, who delighted in loving every dog, as they all grew up and older together. Dawson's family lived in apartments throughout his childhood; no pets allowed. His residence now was of the same ilk. His most consistent form of exercise was of the 'bend the elbow while sitting on a lumpy couch watching other athletes' type.

Consequently, now in the semi-darkness near the lake, Dawson took a large step back as the huge dog with a black and silver lion's mane stood up next to Rinder. A low growl sounding like a small engine rumbled out of the beast's thick chest.

"Careful, Cliffie, Bear here will take you out and bury you like a big bone," Scarlett said softly.

"Nah, he only does that with the bad guys," Rinder said as he pulled Bear's lead back. "Settle down, you big thug, and say hello to Ms. Scarlett." The beautiful beast became a tail-wagging, fairly slobbering puppy before Dawson's shocked eyes as Scarlett knelt briefly, petting and greeting him like an old friend. Turning to Dawson, Rinder's white teeth gleamed in the light of the dim security lamp above the lot. Somehow the deputy's easy manner and broad smile did not make the situation any more comfortable for Dawson.

"Hey, are we gonna be able to feed anybody to our pups tonight or what? We made sure they came hungry."

Dawson shivered, not from the cold, but because of the eerie, downright maniacal laughter of the deputy and his men. They all wore Kevlar protective vests, ready for action and seemed strangely delighted at the prospect of potential danger. Scarlett rose, stood next to Dawson again, and in a few short minutes, she and Dawson briefed Rinder and the squad on the situation at Fortress Fagoli. When they'd finished, Rinder blew out his breath in a frosty cloud.

"The other hostage situation makes it dicey, Scarlett. And dogs versus dogs is never the best plan." He glanced over his shoulder at a young deputy who was crouched down speaking softly into his dog's large, pointed ear. "Hey, Brewskie, whaddya think? Got your 'heat' with ya?"

The young man named Hugo Brewster was called Brewskie by all his colleagues, not only because he brewed his own special beer in his garage, but because he hated the name Hugo so much; the men used it at their own peril. K-9 Deputy Brewskie looked up at his commander and grinned.

"You bet, sir. I'll go fetch it right now, come on, Foster." He'd named his huge German Shepherd after his favorite Australian beer. He and the big animal went off on a quick trot over to one of the sheriff's vans. Dawson could have sworn both of them ran with their tongues hanging out. He frowned as the rest of the squad chuckled and fist-bumped each other, all saying something about "heat".

"What's that about, Rinder?" Dawson asked, "And what other hostage situation?" He glared at Scarlett.

Rinder held up his hand. "Hold on, detective. You'll find out in a minute. Scar, figure it's time to let our friend here in on what ol' Cosmo's about?"

Scarlett nodded, "I gave him a little history on the way up."

Rinder took a deep breath, turned to Dawson and began: "INS, Border Patrol, CHP, and us, we've all been working on this case, undercover as much as possible. Cosmo's been suspected..." He snorted and shook his head in disgust. "Hell, it's no longer just suspicion, we KNOW he's running a human trafficking game. And we figure he holds victims at the Fortress captive until he ships 'em out to whatever godforsaken subhuman creep who's paid for the poor souls. We've been at this for a couple of years, and we're close to nailing his ass, but not close enough. This business with Scarlett's mom and Yano's wife being kidnapped and held may be the doorway to get this fat bastard once and for all. Also, we can finally search the place, and maybe be able to save some others, too. So we gotta use whatever we can that gives us the advantage, and right now, Brewskie's heat may just be what we need." Dawson took all this in, opened his mouth to ask again about the 'heat' but was cut off by Rinder's explanation.

"It's a secret weapon we've used in some bad situations; not often approved of, but what the hell, whatever works."

Brewskie and Foster returned, accompanied by low wolf howls and laughs from the deputies and a lot of nervous action from the tightly held dogs. Rinder clapped the young deputy on the shoulder as he set the large canister affixed with a hose and pump on the ground. "Good boys, both of ya! Now we are in business!"

Brewskie returned to his comrades, his grin matching theirs. Rinder looked at the canister with what seemed like an expression of both love and reverence before he turned to Dawson.

"This, my friend, is 'heat'. It is the scent of a female dog in season condensed in a marvelous liquid which we will spray around the Fortress and make the dogs there very, very uncontrollable and their handlers confused and vulnerable. It was brewed to perfection by our own Deputy Brewskie here. God! I love science!"

"Outstanding, Rinder! Now can we roll on this, please?" Scarlett spat out.

Dawson uneasily nodded his agreement and felt the cold from the damp asphalt creeping into his shoes.

"Sure thing, Missy." Rinder slapped his leather gloved fists together. "Now here's how we're doing this: we'll be on low-volume chatter on our hand-helds. Our dogs have special muzzles also created by our buddy Brewskie here so they can't get the 'heat' scent. Brewskie and Foster will spray in the east area of the compound. Our guys will secure both the dogs and their handlers." He held up his palm towards Dawson as the detective opened his mouth. "Don't worry about how. Like I said, we've had eyes and ears on the Fortress and perimeter for a good while now. When all is secure in that area, we will signal, locked and loaded, and proceed into the Fortress itself. My guys know the layout well, since we have had, shall we say, reason to have quiet chats with Mr. Di Stefano's staff on occasion. Amazing information a couple of good drinks and a promise of immunity will buy. God! We need to get this guy! I'm sure you know how much, detective."

Dawson nodded. "Yeah, we've had to deal with other cases of this nasty 'import business' for some time. Let's do it!"

Rinder nodded, gave his squad a "thumbs up" and suddenly all was in motion. Scarlett and Dawson ran to his car, the now-muzzled dogs were loaded with the deputies in the van and SUV's. Rinder and Brewskie secured their dogs in the back of Rinder's SUV and took the lead.

Scarlett turned to Dawson, her breath fogged the windshield slightly. "So Uncle Cosmo's reputation has interested the SDPD as well?" Dawson quickly rolled down his window. They shivered as the crisp night air blew in. Dawson hunched up his shoulders and glanced quickly at her before he answered, his voice low and tight.

"For some time, we've known Cosmo's been into some kinda drug importing and dealing shit. Gotta be linked in with the Mexican cartel and we're really close on that. Mexican authorities are cooperating more these days and that's good. But that's only one thing. This other thing, this 'slavery'..." He swore and pounded his fist one time on the dashboard.

Scarlett gasped. "God! Everything Lizzie told me was true. When I first approached Rinder with this, he just looked at me, said nothing, so I knew. Oh, hell! Now I know more details than even I suspected. The looks on the faces of the women in the video I got... We really gotta make this stick! Jesus, now I'm more scared than ever about Mom and Lizzie. He *is* the animal I thought he was."

Dawson saw she was trembling, and reached over to turn on the heater. He took a noisy deep breath. "I've never wanted to send anyone to hell before, but this time, I could cheerfully do it, I could, Scarlett."

She looked at him for what seemed like a long time, then looked down at the gun in her hands. When she spoke, there was a slight tremble in her voice but her words were clear. "I get it, but if he lays a hand on my mom, I just might have to call 'dibs' on this one, Cliffie."

This time when he reached out his hand, he did lay it on her knee and to his surprise, she briefly covered it with her own.

"Here's one for ya, Cliffie: 'Sure, forgive your enemies, but first, get even.' Gotta love Cagney." She looked out the window as they approached Fortress Fagoli, the interior lights of the big house shining softly against the shadowy hillside.

CHAPTER THIRTEEN

All motion in the huge living room had stopped. In fact, the very air seemed still for several long seconds after Rosa's attack on Monroe. Her sharp, crystal rosary beads left a string of crimson bumps on his fair cheek. His hand flew to his face. When he pulled it away he was shocked and angered to see the blood. The silver crucifix had cut him below the eye. With a guttural roar he lunged towards the still-scowling Rosa.

"You old bitch! Who do you think ..." But he never finished his sentence. As Rosa took a defensive step back, Lizette screamed and launched herself off the sofa and threw herself at him.

"Don't you touch her, you piece of shit!" She tackled him, her torso flung against his upper body, legs wrapped around him as she used her only weapons, her long acrylic nails and the sharp edge of the plasti-cuffs. She clawed at his already-damaged face, and screamed obscenities.

Taken off balance, Lizette and Monroe toppled to the floor; she straddled him and continued to beat him and scratch him. He struggled to push her off, while trying to protect his face at the same time.

Jeremy was on his feet and moved quickly towards Luca, only to be stopped again by the large gun pointing in his direction. Luca stood, stunned, alternately pointing his weapon at the wrestling duo on the floor and the furious Jeremy, not knowing whether to hit either one. Rosa took advantage of his brief confusion and picked up a piece of the Murano glass fruit from the bowl on the coffee table and threw it as hard as she could at his head. Unfortunately, even without the handicap of being cuffed, Rosa was not blessed with a good throwing arm, so the beautiful glass pear slammed Luca on his chest, bounced off and shattered into a million shining pieces. Luca flinched, whirled on her and shouted. "What the hell? Sit down, you little *strega* or I'll... ."

"You'll what? Shoot an old lady? Oh that's big and brave isn't it? Who brought you up anyway, huh, *bruto!*"

Cosmo and Bruno ran into the room, shouting in unison, "What the hell is going on?"

Monroe had managed to push Lizette off, grab her by her scraped wrists and pin her to the floor. His curly blonde hair fell in front of his eyes and he flicked his head back.

"Godammit, Cosmo, this little whore jumped me and the old lady hit me, too! What good are your goons anyway?"

"Better'n you, Marilyn, since you're the one bleeding and on the floor. Get up, you sorry bastard." Cosmo signaled Bruno and Luca to take charge and walked over to Rosa. Bruno, who was the size of a small room himself, hauled Lizette up off the floor and dumped her, like a rag doll, on the sofa, gun held in one beefy hand, pointing at her enhanced bosom. Jeremy moved towards the big man, bound fists clenched and held high, and clubbed the back of Bruno's thick neck. With speed belying his size, Bruno whirled and fiercely backhanded Jeremy across the jaw. The younger man dropped hard onto his knees. Bruno grabbed the front of Jeremy's shirt and hauled him up onto the sofa with no effort on his part. Jeremy, stunned and in pain, his lip bleeding, wisely held up his hands, palms out as best he could, and sat back, muttering something about big guns meaning small dicks. Bruno's growl silenced him.

Luca pointed his own gun at Rosa advancing on her until she plopped heavily into her chair. She glared at him and made an Italian gesture he knew too well. He glared back: a Sicilian standoff.

"Go clean yourself up, pretty boy." Cosmo addressed Monroe with obvious disdain.

"Talk nice, Uncle C., you still need me." Monroe hissed at him. Before he left, he bent and grabbed Jeremy by the shirt and pulled him close to his face. Jeremy stared back angrily. "That's right, just sit there, you little prick. I'll take care of you later."

Jeremy snarled through clenched teeth. "You promised I'd be okay. You promised me I'd get the car and the condo and now you're just fucking me over. Who's the prick here, huh?"

Monroe's high-pitched bitter laugh made Jeremy sneer back at him. "Little ass! You were just the bait; just somebody to use to get what we wanted. Now you're nothing. Less than nothing. We can throw you to the cops or the wolves, whatever we want. And that goes for you bitches, too." He shoved Jeremy away from him, walked toward the doorway and turned to Cosmo once more. He licked the side of his mouth where Lizette had scratched it, tasting blood. When he spoke his voice was dripping honey.

"Well, Uncle C., all you gotta do now is clean up this mess, I'll take my cut and we're even. I got you what you wanted, so if you'll get my stash ready, I'll be on my way, back to being one of San Diego's finest. Protect and serve, that's me." He waved his hand in a flourish, bowed deeply and sauntered down the hallway.

"Humph!" Rosa said. "That young man is certainly no credit to the police force; that's all I have to say!"

Cosmo looked at her, shook his head in frustration and said, "For the last time, lady, *silenzio*, or else!"

Rosa gave him her sternest look, then awkwardly reached into her pocket, pulled out a tissue and began to wipe the blood off her rosary.

※※※※※

Outside, the dark caravan stopped just on the other side of the fire station, which was about a half mile to the east of the Fortress and nearer the road. Moments later, the men assembled and walked silently through the chaparral towards the big house. Rinder and Brewskie were already at work. Rinder was on the lookout, holding Bear and Foster, both tightly muzzled, their breath snorting through their muzzles making small clouds in the cold dark air. Brewskie sprayed 'heat' on the east perimeter of the compound. Two of the other deputies strung a black trip rope low to the ground in front of the east gate. They'd quickly cut the wires to the electrically charged and controlled gate, disabling it and thereby foiling any attempt of escape by car from the house.

While Cosmo's guard dogs yelped and ran to the scent, the guards followed, calling out to the dogs and each other, cussing and wondering why the main gate didn't open electronically. At Rinder's quiet command, the rest of the squad moved quickly, their night vision goggles giving them a clear view of the action. On cue, Cosmo's guards manually pushed opened the large gate to let the dogs investigate. As they walked out, the deputies pulled the rope. The guards fell, and wisely stayed down when they felt the hot breath of the sheriff's dogs on their faces and the cold muzzles of their owners' guns on their necks.

Brewskie and another deputy put muffling loops along with leashes around Cosmo's guard dogs and secured them into one of the waiting SUV's. They hurried back to the gate, got their own dogs and waited for Rinder's next order. It came quickly and quietly over the hand-helds strapped to their shoulders.

"On my order, Brewskie, take Sloan and Morales and cover the back, see anybody, loose your pups. Lopez, you and Fletcher, take the east side; Dawson, you and I will take the front; Lee and Saunders, take the west side. Same drill; take down who and what you can. But this is a hostage situation, people, take all precautions. Do you copy? *All precautions.* We're gonna move on my regular command. Remember, there may be fireworks. Uncle Cosmo may have other hostages in the attic, so watch yourselves. We want ZERO collateral damage. We need everybody alive, copy that?" There were affirmative answers all around. Scarlett grabbed Rinder's sleeve and spoke in a hoarse whisper.

"What about me? My mother's in there! You gotta let me go with you."

"Oh, hell, no, Scarlett, you're a civilian on this one. No more civilians allowed, we got this, now you stay back or I'll cuff you to the car." Dawson said emphatically and Rinder nodded agreement. She turned on the Deputy.

"Listen, you mutt jockey, I'm the one who got you this far. Let me in, or I'll go on my own!" She started to push forward, but in a swift, practiced motion, Dawson grabbed her and pushed her back against a big oak tree, his hands on her shoulders. The rough bark scratched her back as she struggled against him. Rinder moved in close to the two of them. When he spoke, his voice was soft but there was no mistaking his resolve.

"Scar, you know I know how good you are, but, shit, *Dawson's* not even supposed to be here. Now the CHP will be rolling up soon to close the road, so you stay put and wait for them and let us do OUR jobs."
"Like hell, I will!" Scarlett looked from him to Dawson, her eyes wide with anger and disbelief.

"He's right, Scarlett." Dawson eased up on his grip and nodded at Rinder. Within seconds, the two big men hoisted her up and before she knew it her right hand was cuffed to the handle of Dawson's car. Her indignant cries were stifled by Dawson's sweaty palm clapped on her mouth.

"Stay here and be quiet, goddammit, or I'll gag you, too!"

She shook his hand off and spat her words at both of them. "Both of you are selfish asses! This is MY MOTHER and MY CASE!! Screw this up, and I promise, if you think these dogs are rough and vicious they will be cuddly toothless, clawless puppies compared to *this* bitch!"

Rinder and Dawson let out their collectively held breath. They looked at each other and saw the same frightened look mirrored in their eyes. Rinder shook it off. Bear felt it and woofed quietly.

Before he left her, Dawson crouched down and rolled his flashlight towards Scarlett. "Just in case," he murmured lamely, got up quickly and began to walk away.

"Just in case, what, Cliffie? Think I'm afraid of the dark, you piece of . . ."
Rinder saw Dawson looking back after Scarlett and said, "O.K. Big fella, ready to roll?"

"Ready, let's do it." Dawson responded and turned away from the heat of Scarlett's glare.

Rinder spoke into his hand-held: "All right boys and dogs, let's go. 'Round up the usual suspects.' Now!"

As they all moved out on a quick trot, guns and dogs ready, a surprised Dawson muttered: "Hey, I know that movie...!"

CHAPTER FOURTEEN

It was getting colder by the minute. Scarlett's breath came out in explosive puffs with every cussword. When Rinder and Dawson were out of sight, she strained and reached into the inside pocket of her jacket with her left hand. It took her several minutes, but she retrieved the small tool, and clumsily unlocked the handcuffs.

"Ha!" she muttered. "Pays to be smart *and* well-prepared, boys."

Once free, she walked a few feet, ducked down low behind a thick Manzanita bush, and waited. She took a minute to catch her breath, then ripped off the tape used to dim the flashlight lamp and made her way through the brush to the Fortress. Bent in a low crouch, she shone the now-broadened light on the ground in front of her, taking care to not raise it above her knees.

Breathing hard from exertion and anger, Scarlett stayed close to the west wall of the fortress. Lee and Saunders were already inside the gate. She saw them crouching deeply, making their way towards the house. She slipped by them through the thick brush and circled around to the back. Brewskie, Sloan, and Morales were just up ahead. She held back out of sight, straining to hear their chatter on the hand-helds. Brewskie calmed the dogs while Sloan spoke.

"Sarge, we're in position, near probably a basement door, one step down to it. No security personnel visible. No light coming from this entrance. Advise next move. Over."

Rinder's deep voice cracked a response. "Roger that. We are secured near the front entrance. Got a visual on the front window. Hostages in sight. We count three suspects, three collateral personnel. Suspects are armed, repeat, armed. Do not move until I give the order, repeat, *no movement*. Keep your pups quiet, stay covered and no chatter, on my order. Over."

Scarlett heard all the affirmative answers and watched as the deputies knelt in the dirt, one arm around their dogs' necks whispering to calm them. Only Brewskie wasn't talking to his dog, Foster. He was singing softly in the big dog's fuzzy ear. She watched in astonishment, then smiled as she recognized the old Patsy Cline song, "Crazy". *Whatever works,* she thought, as she heard Foster heave a big, drool-y sigh and lay down at his master's feet.

She figured Rinder had everybody in sight in his night vision binoculars, Bear at quiet attention at his side. He'd never get so close as to endanger civilians. So it was either time to wait or time to move, and she was never good at waiting.

The basement door was behind and to the left of the deputies and dogs. How could she get there without being seen or heard? She looked around for another entrance—there had to be one—but, if she moved, she stood the risk of alerting Brewskie and the others.

Her dad's favorite saying came to mind suddenly: *God hates a coward, kiddo, gotta go for what you want.* Saying a silent prayer to Dad, she began a slow belly crawl away from the waiting squad to the extreme rear of the house. Gritting her teeth, Scarlett tried not to think of what was crawling around in the damp underbrush with her. She inched her way through the brambles and knobby, above ground roots of the low *manzanitas*, praying there was no poison oak around. The smell of smoke from the fireplace in the house mingled with the loamy smell of the dark earth, making her wrinkle her nose. She couldn't risk a sneeze, not now. Then, just to her right about four feet in front of her, the light she held close to her body glinted off something. It was a casement window. Her heart raced as she crept towards it. *Another entrance to the basement!* Holding her breath for an instant, she pulled herself out of the bushes forward. Looking behind her she listened hard. All was quiet; she could make her move now, quickly. On all fours, she moved to the window as fast as she could, set down the flashlight and tried the pull-up handle. It was unlocked! She gave it a yank. It didn't budge. She pulled harder, grunting softly with the effort. This time it opened, but with a squeak so loud she rolled back into the darkness, looking behind her to see if Brewskie or the dogs had heard. Nothing. Pulling the window open as far as she could, Scarlett grabbed the light and pulled her gun out of her pocket. Shining the light into the musty darkness, she saw no signs of life. It was a slight drop to the floor, so she slid in feet first, gun in hand.

"Oooff!" Her sneakered feet hit the tile floor and slipped out from under her. She landed hard on her bottom and sat very still for a minute. No sounds. That was good. Standing up, she thought she saw something large and round in front of her. The flashlight revealed several massive wine barrels and tall racks filled with dusty bottles.

"That little old winemaker, you, huh, Cosmo?" she whispered to herself. *What else you got in here? Too bad I don't have more time to explore. Gotta find the staircase.*

Just then, she heard a thumping sound. Stopping and shining her light carefully around, she strained her ears. Hearing nothing she figured it was just spooky old basement sounds and walked around the barrels towards an opening in the racks. There it was again, the thumping. Turning back towards the barrels, she listened again. It started again, a little louder. Gun in hand, Scarlett cocked her head to one side.

"Oh no, Cosmo, you shithead, not even you would do that!" she said quietly in disbelief. But the thumping was there, in front of her, and it was coming from the wine barrel. Inching around, coming closer to the sound, she reached out and tapped the nearest barrel with the butt of her flashlight. The thumping became frantic, but not from inside the barrel as she first thought. She looked down and shone the light to her left and saw the source of the noise.

Hands and feet bound, bleeding from a raw gash in his shaved head, desperate screams muffled by duct tape across his mouth, Monroe's partner, Detective Jamal Patrick O'Sullivan looked up at Scarlett, his eyes huge with both terror and relief.

❧❦❧❦❧

CHAPTER FIFTEEN

Scarlett stared in shock at O'Sullivan for a few seconds, took a deep breath, then crouched down and grinned at him. "Hey, Irish, what's new?" she said softly. Jamal growled at her and shook his head violently.

"Oh, yeah, here you go." She ripped the tape off his mouth in one quick movement.

"Ahhh! Shit, Salerno. That hurt!"

"Quiet! Want me to put it back? Don't want the goons upstairs to hear us."

"How the hell did you get here, Scarlett? Anybody else with you?" Jamal's voice was harsh and low from disuse.

"Tell you what, Irish, how about you tell me first?" She smiled a little as he pulled back from the Glock pointed at his forehead. Eyes wide, Jamal spoke in a whispered rush.

"Hold it! I'm on your side, remember? I'm the one who told you about the mole and he's here. He's the one got your mama and Lizette and that Blake kid out here. He figures he can use them for some kinda leverage. For what, I don't know." He tilted his head to one side as if waiting for her reaction. She didn't move, and neither did the gun. He sighed and tried again, slower and intense. "Scar, it's Monroe. He's here. He stole your mother's address off Dawson's notepad and gave the information to Cosmo."

"Believable, but still doesn't explain why you're here, Irish. Go ahead, but make it fast and quiet, I've got a hot date upstairs."

"Not unless you've got a small army with you. They don't call this place the Fortress for nothin'. Now untie me, and you can be my backup."

Scarlett snorted a short laugh. "YOUR backup? Not a chance. So if you're not gonna tell me the how and why of your lovely presence here ..." She held up the duct tape again.

"O.K. O.K.. Give me a break here." Jamal squirmed, chaffing at his bonds.

"You and me, we had a deal, remember? I've helped you, right? Monroe's such a weird guy. I thought he couldn't be smart enough to be the mole. But he kept up this thing like he wanted to be in on the Di Stefano case and I got suspicious. I mean, why this case? So I go along with him. He shows me the snitched address and says he wants to check it out. What I don't know is *he* already did, called Cosmo and set it all up. We get there, get out of the car, he comes behind me, sticks his gun in my back and tells me he needs me. Yeah, he needs my dead body to save his own pasty skin! His plan: he delivers Lizette, gets his cut for taking care of Yano and some other bad business. At the same time he makes like he and I are the hot shits following Cosmo. There's a fake shoot-out, Lizette ends up dead, and I end up dead while supposedly trying to help him. Monroe's a little roughed up. Cosmo gets away, of course, but Marilyn's still the big He-ro! Me, his pitiful partner, is now conveniently deceased, while he gets all the credit and a big promotion for solving the case. So he cracks me hard over the head. He and Cosmo's creeps truss me up like a damned pig and pile me into the back of their vehicle; I wake up down here wondering where the hell I am and smelling sour wine. So untie me, dammit, so we can get the son-of-a-bitch!"

Jamal was breathing hard, staring at Scarlett. She looked at him for a few moments, then reached into her pocket for her dad's old pocket knife. Opening it, she said quietly, "O.K. I guess I don't have bunches of choices here, but ..." She curled her index finger behind her thumb and thwacked Jamal hard on the temple with it.

"OW! What the hell is that for?" Jamal glared at her.

"That, my fairly incompetent friend, is for not calling me right away when you suspected your poufy partner. Now my mama is collateral, when she could be home watching her soaps. Jerk!" With a swift movement of the knife, she freed his feet. Just as quickly she cut the rope binding his hands. He rubbed his wrists for a second and tried to stand. Scarlett was already shining her flashlight around looking for the stairwell as Jamal struggled to his feet. "Come on, Irish, haven't got all night."

"Give me a second, my legs kinda fell asleep here." He was bent double flexing his knees.

"Yeah, poor, pitiful you. 'Excuses are like assholes, everybody got one.'" Jamal looked up at her as if to say, "Huh?"

"God, Jamal, you never saw that movie? Thought all *supposed to be* tough guys loved it. Here's the stairs. I don't suppose you have a gun *anymore.*" His nasty look was her answer. "So look around, see if you can find something to hit somebody with, at least. Jeeze, *San Diego's Finest*, my ass."

Jamal stumbled around, grumbling. He emerged from the back of one of the tall wine racks with a huge pipe wrench and a crowbar. "Think this'll do?"

Scarlett grinned at him. "Locked and loaded. Let's go but keep your big feet quiet." Jamal grunted softly at her and started to follow her towards the steep basement stairs. Before they reached the first step, the door opened a crack and Frankie's voice drifted down. Scarlett motioned for them both to duck out of the way of Frankie's line of sight.

"Yeah, I know, I was outside, that's why I wasn't here holding your hand. I'll get a couple of bottles and check on him and be back up in a second. Keep your shirt on, Blondie." Frankie flicked on the light switch above the stairs, closed the door behind him and came down muttering about stupid damned cop traitors. He walked over to the farthest wine rack, pulled out a dusty bottle, mumbling as he wiped off the label. He pulled out another bottle, and seemed satisfied it matched the first.

"Don't drop those, now," came the soft whisper behind him.

Frankie whirled around and found himself face to face with Scarlett and her gun. His eyes widened as he saw Jamal grinning manically behind her.

"How the hell …" Frankie began, but stopped as Scarlett pushed the muzzle of the Glock into his nose. She put her finger to her lips.

"Shhh. Let's be real quiet, shall we? Now, just stand still for a minute, right? Jamal, would you like to relieve our friend here of his weapon, please? Now, I seem to remember your name is Frankie? Am I correct? Just nod, kiddo."

Frankie nodded with difficulty, the gun still pushed against his left nostril. Jamal put down the crowbar and reached around the trembling young man. He pulled the 9 millimeter out of the back of Frankie's belt, checked the clip and smiled. "Don't move now. That's a good boy. Shall we tie our little buddy up, Scar?"

"Nah, I figure it might be nice if he helps us first. You'll give us a hand, won't you, Frankie?"

Frankie started to shake his head, but thought better of it when he saw the cold look in Scarlett's eyes. He stood stock still while she spoke, her voice a harsh whisper.

"Now listen, you little creeplet, that's MY MAMA you have upstairs, so this is how we're gonna play nice. You go upstairs with us, help us get Monroe, then we go and get Mama and Lizette. Oh? You look skeptical. Not a good look for you." She pushed the gun farther up his nose, causing him to push his head backward at a painful angle. She continued. "Frankie, I'm gonna make contact with some friends as soon as we get our friend Monroe secured. And then all the cops and mad doggies in the world are gonna come down on you, Cosmo and your little house party. Just so you know, before I do that, if you don't cooperate with us, well, you'll see that I love my mama so much, I'd have no problem taking you out. *Capice?*" From the way Frankie's eyes bulged, she knew she'd made her point and nodded to Jamal.

Being as still as he could, Frankie looked warily as Jamal came around and took the wine from him. Scarlett backed off. Before Frankie could reach up to rub his nose, Jamal, gun in hand, landed a painful right cross on his jaw, sending the young man to his knees.

"That's just for the hell of it. Oh, and maybe for tying me up. Now let's get up the stairs and find my lovely partner." He grabbed Frankie by the hair and hauled him roughly to his feet. With no amount of persuasion at all, Frankie told Scarlett and Jamal not only that Monroe was in the kitchen drinking but in a few short minutes gave them a rough floor plan description of the first floor of the Fortress. Armed with the information they needed, the trio made their way cautiously up the stairs. Jamal pushed Frankie up ahead of him, Scarlett followed close behind. As soon as Frankie pushed the door open, Monroe called out. His voice carried down the hallway from the kitchen.

"'Bout time, you little flake. What the hell were you doing? Squeezing the damned grapes yourself?" His tirade was cut short when he saw Jamal standing behind the perspiring Frankie. Monroe's hand went for his gun in his shoulder holster, then he froze.

"Wouldn't try that, Goldilocks." Scarlett had come quickly around through the dark hallway and dining room into the kitchen behind him. Monroe was greedy, but he wasn't stupid. He put both hands in the air when he felt her cold gun muzzle beneath his ear.

"Now that's a smart cop, a dirty cop, but smart enough to know when he's out-gunned. You prick!" Jamal spoke softly, but there was no mistaking the venom in his voice. Monroe sneered at his partner, as Scarlett reached around and took his gun.

"Why, Irish, Sweetie, how clever of you to get yourself loose. Oh wait, I see, you had help. Well, I should have known you couldn't accomplish much by your little self."

Jamal growled at Monroe, pushed Frankie aside and charged at his partner. Before he could reach him, Scarlett brought her gun down hard on Monroe's blonde head with a solid "crack". The tall policeman's knees buckled and he grabbed the edge of the kitchen counter before he could fall.

"God!" he exclaimed.

Jamal was next to Monroe in an instant, had a handful of his golden hair, and pushed his face into the granite countertop.

"Shut the fuck up, Monroe," he growled. "Believe me, I could cheerfully take you out right now and not give a damn."

"Yep, and Frankie and I would be the witnesses to it being self-defense, wouldn't we Frankie boy?" Scarlett whispered hoarsely into Monroe's bleeding ear. Monroe stopped struggling. He was beat and he knew it. Frankie stood paralyzed against the wall, his eyes wide.

Scarlett straightened up and looked at the young man. "Frankie, you are not cut out for this life, kid. Now, how many people are there with guns in the living room? And remember to speak softly or you might get hit again, huh?" Just to make sure, Scarlett reached over and turned on the small CD player near the refrigerator. She smiled as the Puccini opera aria floated across the room. She went over to the door, but no one outside the kitchen seemed to hear or care.

Frankie reached his hand up and wiped the sweat off his upper lip. His voice was barely above a whisper. "Uh, there's Uncle Cosmo, Bruno and Luca. You don't want to mess with Bruno. He's pretty mean, most of the time."

"I'll make a note of that. Okay, that makes three guns to two. Time to call in the cavalry." She reached in her back jeans pocket and pulled out her cell phone.

"Frankie, are you still working on that 'shit for brains' certificate or do you think you can take down a text I'll dictate to you? Kinda need my hand free for gun and such here."

Frankie nodded a quick agreement and she set up the phone and handed it to him.

Outside, Rinder's phone vibrated in his pocket. "Yeah, Rinder here," he answered softly. He listened for a moment, never taking his eyes off the window in front of him. The scene had quieted down considerably.

"Hey. Davison here. CHP has landed. There are four of us working our way up the hill to assist when you're ready."

"Roger that, Davison. Got a P.I. friend cuffed to an unmarked SDPD car just at the left of the drive near a grove of *manzanitas*. She's clean. Did you spot her yet?"

Dawson listened closely to the exchange. Davison's response made him feel colder than ever.

"Negative, Rinder. Hold on a sec." He could hear Davison breathing into the phone before he answered. "Nobody there, cuffs on the ground. Who are we looking for?"

"God dammit! It's Salerno, Scarlett Salerno. We kept her away from the action. She was supposed to hook up with you guys and wait."

"Nope, no sign of the lady."

Dawson swore under his breath and shook his head. "I fuckin' knew it! Should've chained her hand and foot to the damned car!"

The puzzled deputy turned to look at him, but said nothing. Just then, Dawson's cell phone buzzed. Text message. He dropped the phone when he read it. "Goddamned stupid hot-dogging woman!" He spat out.

Rinder picked up the phone, read the message and muttered, "How the hell?" He handed the phone back to Dawson who was checking his weapon for the fiftieth time that night. Hoping he'd read it wrong, looked at the message again. No, he'd read it right the first time, but a second reading didn't make him any happier. He cursed again as his eyes swept over the words.

"Hi, Cliffie. Check out the front window. Wanna join us?"

They both looked up just as Scarlett, Jamal, Frankie and Monroe entered the living room. Jamal's gun was on Monroe, Scarlett's pointed at the hapless Frankie's head.

Dawson sputtered a "God Damn—Monroe, Jamal, how?"

It was like watching a movie, but a bad one. Within minutes, the scene changed, Monroe threw himself bodily across the room towards Rosa. He landed hard on the floor at Jeremy's feet. Jeremy quickly took the advantage and aimed a kick at Monroe's head. But Monroe's cop instincts were faster than Jeremy's attempt so he rolled away from Jeremy's alligator-booted foot before it could reach its mark. Scarlett pushed Frankie out of the way and pointed both her gun and Monroe's confiscated one at Luca. He in turn raised his semi-automatic at Jamal and Scarlett. Bruno snatched Rosa out of her chair and held his gun to her head. Rosa twisted around and flailed at Bruno. She was so short the best she could do was whip her rosary around, aiming at his head. Bruno tried to duck the sharp crystal beads while trying to hold her tight. He cursed loudly as she stomped repeatedly on his foot, but didn't let go. Cosmo grabbed Monroe, hefted him to his feet and smacked him across the face. Everyone with a gun was shouting to each other to put their guns down. Lizette screamed and stood on the red couch, jumping up and down. Screaming and jumping, she looked like she was on a trampoline in a horror movie.

Stunned, yet somehow sounding amused, Rinder spoke clearly into his hand-held. "O.K. boys and pups, let's make a nice, quiet but effective entrance, shall we? Remember, we've got hostages and crazy people with guns, lots of 'em. YeeeeHawwww!"

CHAPTER SIXTEEN

Like a small stealth army squad, Rinder's men and their dogs moved toward the house. With so much yelling and confusion in the living room, no one heard the back and side doors being forced open. Rinder and Dawson crept up the stairs leading to the deck and the front door. Crouching low, Rinder barked, "Now!" into the hand-held. He kicked open the front door and loosed his giant dog, Bear, shouting "Gun!" in the dog's ear. In an instant, Bear leapt into the room, launched his big furry frame, teeth bared, at the first gun he saw. At the same time, Brewskie, Sloan and Morales and their dogs came running in from the hallway and all was chaos. Scarlett shouted as soon as she saw Bear fly at the startled Bruno.

"Mama! Hit the deck!" She fell to the floor and rolled into a ball. The dogs went after any gun they saw, clamping their jaws on the hands holding them. Between the snarling of the dogs, the deputies shouting for everyone to get down, Bruno, Luca and Monroe screaming in pain, Lizette's maniacal screeching, Jeremy's cursing while throwing wild kicks at the fallen Luca, and Rosa's cheering, the combined noise was ear-splitting.

Dawson grabbed Rosa's arm and pulled her away from the melee. "Get down behind here!" He shouted in her ear as he pulled her further down behind the large wingchair.

"Look out! Cliff, behind you!" Scarlett shouted.

Dawson looked around just in time to see Cosmo looming over him with a large brass candlestick ready to come down on his head. Crouching and ducking quickly, he tackled Cosmo hard at the knees. Cosmo's size and the force of the tackle propelled them both through the large window and onto the deck below. The glass shattering crash succeeded in silencing the room. The deputies gave their dogs the "Hold" command and quickly relieved their moaning captives of their guns. Scarlett ran to the empty window frame and looked out. Dawson and Cosmo were on the deck, glass all around them; neither of them moving. Seeing that Rosa was still safely behind the chair, she went out the door, hurried down the steps to the deck. By the time she got there, Cosmo had rolled away from the still-inert Dawson and was reaching for the detective's gun.

"Don't do it, Cosmo!" Scarlett was on the last step, the Glock aimed at his head.

He swung his hand around, it was bleeding from cuts, but the gun he held was steady. "You don't have the guts, you stupid bitch."

Just as he raised the gun to fire, Dawson lurched up to his knees and pushed him. The shot went wild into the trees causing a large snowy white owl to take noisy flight into the darkness. Cosmo whirled on Dawson, turning the gun on him. Dawson ducked, as another shot rang out. He looked down to see where he was hit, just as Cosmo groaned and fell face first onto the redwood planks, blood oozing from his left shoulder. Dawson struggled to his feet as Scarlett reached him, the Glock still warm in her shaking hand.

"Cliff, you're bleeding. Are you all right?"

"What?" Dawson looked down as Scarlett pulled his jacket away from his shirt. The red circle was growing rapidly around the large shard of glass imbedded in his side.

"Shit!" he said weakly, sitting back hard on the deck.

"Stay still, Cliffie, for God's sake! I'll get help." She helped him lie back on the cold wood then took off her own jacket and put it under his head. Running towards the steps, she shouted into the open door. "Rinder! Dawson's down! Need some help out here." Rosa and Rinder, having heard the shots, were already heading down towards her.

"*Bella Mia*, are you all right?" Rosa elbowed the startled deputy out of the way and reached Scarlett first.

"Yeah, but, Cliff's not."

Rinder was already calling for EMT's. "They'll be here soon, just hold on," he said to Dawson just as Brewskie shouted down through the broken window.

"Hey, Sarge! We got everything secured down here. Morales and I are heading upstairs with Frankie to check out a few 'extra' guests in the house. I've checked with our CHP guys and they're rolling here right now. Whooee, seems like everybody in the house wants to talk to us, now we got our pups in charge."

"Be up in a second. Thanks, Brewskie." Rinder turned back to Scarlett and Dawson. She was kneeling on the deck next to the detective, her hands pressed against his bleeding side. Rosa was muttering Hail Marys as Rinder acknowledged the response from the EMT's. He bent down and spoke to Dawson.

"Hey, man, the guys are heading up the road now, you'll be okay. They'll fix you up."

Dawson gave him a shaky smile. "Thanks. No worries, just a little scrape.

How's Uncle Cosmo?"

Rinder poked Cosmo's prone figure in the side with his boot. Cosmo emitted a low groan but didn't move. "He'll live, I guess. We'll have the medical guys fix you first. Priorities, ya know." He grinned down at Dawson and Scarlett, loosened his flack jacket enough to be able to reach into his shirt pocket and pulled out a somewhat smashed cigar. He always had one, but never lit it; just a celebratory gesture he was known for. Jamming it between his teeth, he spoke around it.

"Well, looks like our work here is almost done, Tonto. Gotta go check on my boys' progress. Here come the reinforcements." He swiftly freed Rosa's hands, put his fingers to his forehead in a snappy salute, and went back up the steps.

Sirens sounded in the distance. Red lights and headlights shone as the CHP rolled up the driveway, the paramedic wagon close behind.

Rosa bent down slightly to Dawson and Scarlett. "They're just about here, *Bella Mia*. How's he doing?"
Scarlett looked at Dawson's pale face. His forehead was dotted with perspiration. "You heard Mama, Cliffie. How goes it?"

Dawson blew out a long breath, raised his head slightly and grimaced as he saw the glass sticking out at an angle from his gold shirt. "That's pretty much it for this shirt, I guess." He tried a laugh, but it turned into a groan.

Scarlett grinned. "Lucky thing, 'cause that is one butt-ugly shirt, and tie, and suit …"

"Cut me some slack, will ya, Salerno?" Looking down at the blood-soaked cloth, then up at Scarlett, they both laughed at his unintentional but still terrible pun regarding his sad attire. Dawson winced at the pain as he put his head back down. The sirens stopped short as the paramedic van pulled up below the deck.

Rosa shook her head at the two of them. "Honestly, how can you two laugh after all that's happened?" She straightened, put her hands on the small of her back and groaned. "You know, Scarlett, honey, maybe you should get another job or maybe somebody else to help you."

"Huh? Why?"

"Because, *Figlia Mia*, 'I'm getting too old for this shit'."

Dawson groaned loudly and not from the pain in his side this time. Rosa looked down at him and frowned. "What's the matter, detective? You think my daughter's the only one who likes movies?"
Upstairs in the attic, Galina and Malaya heard the uproar downstairs. Malaya started to go to the window, but Galina pulled her back.

"No! I think there is shooting. We must stay away from the door and window." She pulled the trembling Malaya back against the wall by the cots. Almost as quickly as it had begun, the noise from below quieted down. Straining to hear, Galina could only make out loud voices. Then suddenly there were footfalls pounding up the stairs.

Malaya cried out softly. "Sweet Jesus, please don't let them kill us!"

Galina looked around for something, anything to defend them with. She grabbed the wooden chair and held it in front of her like a lion tamer. Slowly she walked towards the door, hearing deep voices as the footsteps came closer.

One of the voices said gruffly, "Come on, scum, get that key working."

The second voice Galina recognized as Frankie, the young man who had at least seemed kinder than the other horrible men who'd kept them captive. But this was no time to be cautious, so she kept her grip on the chair and advanced to the door, prepared to thrust it at whoever she saw first. The knob turned, the door was opened slowly and she charged, roaring like the she-cat she was named for.

"Whoa!" Frankie jumped back when he saw Galina's lips pulled back in a feral snarl. He caught himself before he fell down the steep stairs, as Brewskie quickly stepped forward and grabbed the legs of the chair, pulling Galina off balance. She dropped the chair and, screaming, lunged at Brewskie. In her weakened state, his reflexes were better than hers and he simply grabbed her, pinning her arms to her sides.

She thrashed around, trying to twist out of his grasp as he shouted at her.

"Hold on, Miss! We're tryin' to help. We're here to get you outta here!" Brewskie had to side step as she tried to kick him. Frankie came forward and tried to calm her.

"Galina! Stop! It's over, he's the cops, and you're, uh, rescued. Get it?"

She was breathing hard, tears streaming down her cheeks. Looking at Frankie, she stopped struggling and heard Malaya sobbing behind her.

"Oh, my sweet Lord, we are saved!"

Hearing this, Galina looked into Brewskie's deep, blue eyes, and saw him nod slowly.

"That's right, m'am, we're the good guys. You done been saved."

Galina's legs suddenly felt like rubber, and she began to slide to the floor. Brewskie held onto her so she slipped to the floor slowly and spoke in her ear with the same soft voice he used to calm his dog. Galina sobbed softly, hugged her savior and thought she'd never heard such a beautiful sound in all her life.

⚜⚜⚜⚜⚜

Two days later, Scarlett walked into Dawson's hospital room just as Chief Chang was leaving. As they passed each other, Chang gave Scarlett a hard look and a curt nod.

"Wow, Cliffie, your boss just gave me what Mama would call the *malocchio*, you know, the evil eye. What's that about?" She put the plastic container she

91

held down on his bed tray.

"Gosh, Salerno, I have no idea. Maybe he's just suspicious of lady dicks."

"Ha, Ha. So howareya? How's the ouchie?"

He batted her hand away as she reached to pull the sheet away. "It's fine, thanks. I should be outta here tomorrow."

"That's great. Hey, how about the double bust on Cosmo and his bunch! Wow, he rolled over on Monroe so we got that dirty mole for murder-one. AND we got Cosmo for conspiracy to commit murder and murder for hire, AND we got him for the human trafficking gig. AND the captives we found in the attic rooms have been treated and are safe in the women's shelter downtown, operated by the Good Sisters of Social Service—thanks to Mama's friends there. They gave great intel to your guys about the big yellow house and where the other workers lived as well."

Dawson nodded. "Yeah, the big raid there garnered so much evidence, Cosmo and his bunch will gone for a very long time." He frowned. "Somehow we didn't get all the staff, ya know. Cap says according to the ladies we freed there's a woman who was Cosmo's right hand; kinda in charge of that operation and more. We didn't get her and didn't get a couple of the 'recruiters' he used. They're still out there somewhere. Too bad.

Scarlett gave him a twisted smile. "Francesca Madonna Cavalcante, that's the bitch we still haven't got. If she's as smart as everybody involved said, I'm betting she hopped a private flight to Italy or Morocco or somewhere we can't get to her, *yet*." Dawson raised an inquisitive eyebrow at this, but Scarlett just ignored his unvoiced question and continued. "I'm doing some *pro-bono* investigating to locate sponsors and family members of the two ladies. The little one is gonna head to San Francisco to her Auntie's, and I might be able to get her into school, like she wanted. As for the Russian girl, she doesn't want to go back, understandably, so with a sponsor, she can remain and look for a job. Lizette is gonna live very securely and nicely in the witness protection program after she testifies; have no idea where, but that's the point, right? Good work all the way around, if I do say so." She raised her fist for a bump, but he didn't return it.

"Yeah, Cosmo, his bunch, and Monroe are gonna spend a lot of time in 9-by-12 suites at the gray brick resort, but seems to me you got the better part of the deal." He grumbled and picked at his covers.

Scarlett frowned and plopped down on the bed at his feet, ignoring his wince. "Why so, Cliffie? Oh, is it because of the money? Is that it? Now you know that was my deal with Lizette all along. I find out what Yano was up to and proved he broke the pre-nup, so I got the big check, thanks to great work by my lawyer buddies. What's the big deal? You got the credit for finding Monroe, the mole, didn't you? I thought I made that clear to ugly old Chang."

Dawson sighed and rubbed his side. "Yeah, matter of fact, that's why Chang was here." He looked down and spoke softly, a blush creeping over his face and onto his bald pate. "Looks like I'm in for a commendation, promotion to Detective 1st and, well, a raise. 'Cause of, you know, the Monroe thing and stuff. So I guess I owe ya, Salerno."

Scarlett whooped and bounced up and down on the bed, causing Dawson to yelp and hold his side. "Oh, sorry, Cliffie! I'm just so excited for you. That's great news. And hey, you don't owe me nothin'. Wasn't for you, my mama would've been, well…" Her voice trailed off and they looked at each other for a long, awkward moment. "So let's call it even, O.K."

He gave her a crooked smile and cleared his throat. "Deal. Now what's in the box?"

"Oh, yeah, almost forgot. Mama made cannolis for you." She opened the box, pulled out a tiny plate, and put a fresh cannoli on it, and handed it to him as if it were a sacred object. "These are the BEST you will ever eat, guaranteed." She smiled and nodded in anticipation of his reaction.

Dawson picked up the cannoli carefully and took a bite. His eyes bugged with pleasant surprise as he tasted the rich, flaky crust, and the smooth, creamy filling. "Oh my God, Scar!" he mumbled around a glorious mouthful. "These things should be illegal." He devoured the rest of the confection and licked his fingers. He grinned when he saw there were three more in the container. Scarlett nodded and smiled back at him.

As he wiped his mouth with the napkin she handed him, he shook his head and said, "You know, this could be the beginning of a beautiful friendship."

Scarlett's eyes widened. She laughed with complete delight. "Cliffie, do you mean it? Or are you just quoting the movie? You and me, a beautiful friendship?"

"Nah, I just meant me, your mama, and the cannoli."

✿✿✿✿✿

EPILOGUE

Scarlett took a sip of the deliciously potent black coffee and smiled. The morning sun on the terrace was warm on her shoulders. She inhaled deeply. The air was clean and fresh with a slight scent of rosemary and rich loamy earth from the herb garden below. The apartment was on the upper floor an old house. Their landlady cultivated vegetables and herbs for herself and her tenants. They made every meal an exquisite adventure. Picking up the letter she'd brought with her, she slit open the envelope with a table knife and began to read.

My dear friend Scarlett,

How I love your name! I hope this find you well and you forgive my bad English. I am learning to write better. The night school here helps me. Here! Here am I at last in the city I dream about for long time. Hollywood! Well, close, yes? Universal City is neighbor to Hollywood. I see sign each day.

My job here at restaurant Hard Rock Hollywood is so close to Universal Studios. When I have day off, I walk and walk all around and sometimes even go to Studios for fun. But I save my money, just like you advise. I go to classes to be better in English, yes, but also to learn to become U.S. Citizen! Yes, my friend—a surprise for you! I wish to be American. Maybe someday I get to work in big movie studio, even. I take your good advice, yes??

Family I stay with, like you say, are good people. They run from Russia like me, but have better luck since they educated and able to get good work in international law firm here. They understand me and treat me like daughter. I am so grateful I have such good sponsors. (That is right word, yes?) I have nice room of my own and am learning much from them.

I talk on phone each week with Malaya. She sends you much love from San Francisco. Her nursing school is very hard, she says, but she so happy. Auntie she live with is good to her. She sleeps in real bed in her own room, not on lumpy sofa like before. Like me, she is so grateful to you for help and for the extra money you give us both to get what you say is fresh start. She will write soon, she promise.

94

Malaya say she pray for you and your mama every night. I not good at praying, but I send good wishes and thoughts to you both always. Never will I be able to thank you for all you do for us. You save our lives and so we all belong to each other somehow. Is that how you think, too? I hope so. I must go now so letter will be mailed before my work begins. I hope you enjoy yourself and I will write again. Maybe better English next time?

Malaya says God Bless You all the time. I think that is right thing to say to you now.

Your Friend,
Galina

"Hey, *Bella Mia!* Are we going to go shopping on the Ponte Vecchio or what? I'd like to see the Pitti Palace today, too? Are you going to get ready, huh?" Rosa came out on the terrace, purse in hand, sun hat at a jaunty angle on her silvery head.

Scarlet smiled, folded the letter and put it back in the envelope and stood. "Yep, Mama, I'll get ready, but you know, the best *gelataria* here in Florence is right by the Ponte Vecchio. Might just have to stop there first." Seeing the letter and the return address, Rosa looked up at Scarlett, brow furrowed. "Was it all worth it, Honey? They'll be okay, right?" She came to stand next to her daughter.

"Yes, they're fine. And yes, it was worth it."

Together they looked over the red tiled roofs of Florence. The bells at the *Duomo* rang in the distance. Rosa grasped her daughter's hand, sighed and said. "*Grazie, Bella Mia. Ti Voglio Bene.*"

Kissing her mother's small hand, Scarlett replied, "I love you, too, Mama."

She picked up the letter and her espresso cup and began to follow Rosa into the living room of the apartment when her cell phone began to buzz. She glanced down at the caller's name.

"*Andiamo, Figlia Mia! (Let's go, my daughter!)*" Rosa called from inside.

"*Adesso*, Mama, *Adesso! (Now!)*" She pushed 'decline' on the screen, turned off the phone, smiled once more at the rooftops of Florence and hurried inside.

AFTERWORD

This is a work of fiction, meant to entertain. However, I hope it enlightens, in some small way, the readers to the horrific crime and practice of Human Trafficking. This dreadful practice is happening all over the world and the United States is not immune to its evil. The 'Task Force' mentioned in this work was real, as was the, at the time, lukewarm response. Today, we know there are many people here in the U.S. and all over the world who have come to realize the importance of fighting to stop this horrendous exploitation of both adults and children.

As I was writing this short novel, Assembly Speaker Toni Atkins of California introduced legislation to provide housing for sexually exploited children and ensure state agencies collaborate to stop this crime. I quote Speaker Atkins:

> *Human trafficking is modern day slavery and, unfortunately, this crime is growing rapidly in our state. According to the FBI, the San Francisco, Los Angeles and San Diego metropolitan areas comprise three of the nation's 13 areas of 'high intensity' child sex trafficking exploitation in the country. Victims of human trafficking are some of our most vulnerable members of society, and we cannot allow this injustice to continue.*

The report that I refer to in the book is entitled: 'Executive Summary: Human Trafficking in California'. In it is stated the many forms of trafficking and their victims, who are not just children, but also adolescents and adults working in what is tantamount to forced labor in many fields, as the characters of Malaya and Galina. Many of these victims are undocumented immigrants, promised a better life by the smugglers who brought them here for their own financial gain.

In September 2005, California enacted its first anti-trafficking law. (Assembly Bill 22, Lieber) to make any form of human trafficking a felony in this state and assist victims in rebuilding their lives. I thank the Legislators of my home state for taking such positive action in combating this horrible crime and urge all citizens of our country to encourage lawmakers to put an end to this modern day practice of slavery.

Many thanks also to Thornton Sully and the crew at A Word with You Press. I'm grateful for the guidance, interest and PATIENCE you have shown me and Ms. Scarlett as we took this slow journey together.

And always, my greatest thanks, appreciation and love to my husband and soul mate, Jim Keeley, for his encouragement and belief in me.

Ti amero per sempre!

This could be the continuation of a beautiful relationship...

Scarlett avoids trouble as much as she avoids Rosa's cannoli. Here is a taste of her next misadventure...

Take a seat!

Graciella started a new 500 piece jigsaw puzzle the same way every time. She was a patient woman who liked to challenge herself.

She didn't begin the process by looking for corners like many people would. No, Graciella spread all the pieces on her special table in her modest parlor and would simply leave them there in their colorful, misshaped disarray for several days. She'd pass by each day on her way to some other task, look down at the pieces for a time, pick up one or two pieces, study them, turn them around in her fingers and sometimes set them aside together at one end of the table. There they would sit alone like forgotten acquaintances. This distinctive process would go on for a week, a month, perhaps longer. Graciella never rushed anything.

"To rush is the sure path to mistakes," she'd often say.

This table has only this use. Everyone she knew, her family, friends, business associates, even her fat, decidedly ugly yellow-eyed cat, Ludovico, knew that they disturbed the table at their great peril. Yes, Graciella was a patient, consistent woman, but one known very well in her province here in Sicily and not just for her talent in solving jigsaw puzzles.

❦❦❦❦❦

Scarlett's phone buzzed again. She looked at it, pressed the decline button and took another spoonful of her delicious chocolate hazelnut gelato. She smiled as she watched her mother, Rosa, happily attack her own gelato, eyes closed in gelato-coma rapture.

"*Dio Mio*, this IS the best gelato in Florence, no doubt!"

"Yep! You know I wouldn't steer my Mama wrong. Mmmmmmmm!"

They sat in contented silence for a few delicious minutes. Couples strolled down the arched bridge of the Ponte Vecchio, arms around each other, smiling and chatting. The late afternoon sun shone on the lazy Arno below as small rowboats glided by and young men and women in two-person kayaks raced along, calling out cheerful challenges as they passed each other. Scarlett finished her gelato, sighed and closed her eyes, thinking she had possibly never felt so completely at peace.

"*Scusiami, Signorina, Signora.*" Scarlett sat bolt upright. A deep insistent voice pulled her right back into her professional "on alert" mode. Rosa's

Mama Instinct felt the tension in her daughter's posture and went into action.

"*Cosa vuoi, Signore?*" She sat up straight and glared at the intrusive man. It took her a second or two to realize he was in a policeman's uniform and the warm Florentine sun suddenly turned cold. The officer ignored her question, and only faced Scarlett.

"*Sei Signorino Scarlett Salerno?*" His tone was all business, his intense dark eyes moving from the notebook in his hand to her face. Scarlett saw her mother pale and then her protective mode rose in a minute and she knew her Italian would fail her, so she improvised.

"*Ufficiale, Englise per favore.* What do you want?" She put her hand out on the table towards her mother as a sign that she had this.

The officer answered her in polite and very good English, which irritated Scarlett.

"*Permisso*, I am Officer Gianni Greco. My *supervisore* has need to speak with you."

Scarlett felt the heat rise in her face. "Your supervisor? What is this about, why do the Florentine police want to speak with me? I'm here with my mother on vacation. Am I being charged with something? No, Officer Greco, I see no need to go with you at all."

The officer sighed deeply and quietly asked for her passport. Scarlett balked until another, very tall, large officer with a dark visage and a hefty unibrow walked up to join Officer Greco. Rosa became more disturbed and began speaking in a combination of fast Sicilian dialect and English. Officer Greco addressed both the women in calm tone, one hand palm down, gesturing for both of them to settle. Scarlett had a cold lump in her stomach that had nothing to do with her gelato. Placing her hand on Rosa's, she shook her head.

"*Calma*, Mama. It's okay, I'll find out what this is about." She dug in her purse and handed Greco her passport. He looked at it carefully, compared it to his notes. Without handing it back to her, he put it in his shirt pocket and spoke quietly, noticing they were being watched by people around them. "Please, *Signorina, Signora*, come with me. I promise you there is no trouble for either of you."

Rosa stood, definitely not calm; "*Per Che?* Why did something happen to Catherine and Evan? What's going on?"

Again, Scarlett and Greco spoke softly, trying to calm her. Scarlett went to Rosa and put her arm around her shoulders. "Officer, my sister and her husband are in the U.S., but will be traveling to Italy in a few weeks to join us. Is this about them, are they safe?"

Greco came close to both of them. "*Signora, Signorina*, I promise no harm has come to your family. We have been looking for you and I am under the strictest orders to bring you to my supervisor. I can only tell you it is a matter of great, even international importance. Believe me, *Signorina* Salerno, all this will make sense when we are at the station and my superior can explain. We must avoid a scene! If only you had answered your telephone!"

Scarlett closed her eyes, gave her mother's shoulder a gentle squeeze and said, 'Just when I thought I was out, they pull me back in."

ABOUT THE AUTHOR

Mary L. Keeley was born in New Orleans, but has lived in San Diego, California since early childhood.

Her lifelong love of books began when her big sister, Pat, taught her to read at a very young age. In fact she has no memory of NOT being able to read. The love of motion pictures came also at a young age, as soon as she was judged old enough to walk to the neighborhood Crest Theater on University Avenue in East San Diego. The theater is long gone, and the neighborhood is now called University Heights, but the memory and fascination with cinema remains. Those Saturday Matinees definitely contributed to both her imagination and her love of good writing, snappy dialog and the sassy dames who spit out those great lines.

Always desiring to write herself, Mary loved any writing assignment given in school and is grateful to the teachers who encouraged and appreciated her efforts. Marriage and raising 4 wonderful sons often put writing literally on the shelf. Fortunately Mary's work often kept her writing, but in a different mode. She has written for in house publications for San Diego County Library as well as reviews for documentary films made specifically for libraries. She has been published in Westways Magazine and has self-published a short memoir entitled "Time in the Middle" about traveling by car across country from 1955 to 1963, before the time of completed interstate highways AND videos in cars that kept kids occupied. She has written a yet unpublished novel set in Ireland, which has absolutely no reference at all to motion pictures, but there may be a few ghosts lingering about.

Frankly, My Detective is her first published novel.

A word about...

A Word with You Press
Editors and Advocates of Fine Stories in the Digital Age

A Word with You Press is a playful, passionate, and prolific consortium of writers, editors, designers and publishers who have been helping authors like yourself achieve their goals since 2009. We are drawn to the notion that nothing is more beautiful or powerful than a story well told. We help you tell it.

Writers and artists don't just happen; they are created by nurturing, mentoring, and by damn good editing. We provide this literary triad through our interactive website, www.awordwithyoupress.com. Our regular writing contests give you an opportunity to hone your skills, and get both professional and peer feedback, as your entries are published on the site and invite commentary.

We have helped first-time authors become award-winners, and we, ourselves, have won awards for writing, editing, and publishing excellence.

The first step to writing your novel? Intent. If you've got it, let's talk. Send inquiries to Thornton Sully, at thorn@awordwithyoupress.com

Thornton Sully has Jack-Londoned his way across the globe (most recently, Prague) sleeping with whatever country would have him, and picking up stray stories along the way. A litter of dog-eared passports that have taken up residence in his sock drawer are a constant temptation.

A Word with You Press
Publishers & Purveyors of Fine Stories in the Digital Age

Available or coming soon from

A Word with You Press

Almost Avalon
by Thornton Sully

A young couple struggles with love and life on the island
frontier just twenty-six miles west of Los Angeles.

The Mason Key
Volume One
A John Mason Adventure
by David Folz

A street urchin in England, around the time the Colonies declare
independence, cheats the hangman to begin this historical adventure series.
He discovers that his father's death may not have been an accident at all,
but part of a broader conspiracy.

The Mason Key II
Aloft and Alow
A John Mason Adventure
by David Folz

The historical saga continues as young Mason becomes
a mid-shipman on the very ship on which he was as
stow-away at the conclusion of *The Mason Key, Volume One.*

The Mason Key III
The Return
A John Mason Adventure
by David Folz

Mason and Marie fend off pirates en-route to her father's plantation. John struggles with the Third Principle, Honor, and the Cruelty of Slavery while making his way back home.

Angus MacDream and the Roktopus Rogue
by Isabelle Rooney-Freedman

Young adults on a mythical Scottish island save the world. Delightfully illustrated by Teri Rider.

The Coffee Shop Chronicles, Vol. I,
Oh, the Places I Have Bean!

An anthology of award-winning stories inspired by events that occurred over a cup of coffee.

The Coffee Shop Chronicles, Vol. II,
A Jolt of Espresso

Stories condensed to exactly 100 words each, inspired by our favorite brew.

The Courtesans of God
by Thornton Sully

A novel based on the real life of a temple priestess in the palace of the King of Malaysia.

Left Unlatched
in the hopes that you'll come in…
A Book of Poetry by R.T. Sedgwick
Winner of the 2012 San Diego Book Awards – Poetry.

The Sky is Not the Limit
And other selected poems
The second volume of poems by R.T. Sedgwick

The Gift of an Imaginary Girl
Coco and Other Stories
by award-winning writer Kristy Webster

The magical-realist tale of a girl whose deformity
changes a whole village.

The Boy with a Torn Hat
by Thornton Sully
Finalist in the 2010 USA Book Awards for Literary Fiction

"Henry Miller meets Bob Dylan in this coming of age romp played out
in the twisted alleyways and smoky beer halls of Heidelberg. Sully is a
cunning wordsmith and master of bringing music to art and art to language.
Excessive, expressive, lusty, and once in a blue metaphor—profound. Here
is what I mean: 'Some women are imprisoned like a tongue in a bell—they
swing violently but unnoticed until the moment of contact with the bronze
perimeter of their existence—and then the sound they make astonishes us
its power and pain and beauty, and its immediacy' — Wunderbar"
—Jonathan Freedman, Pulitzer Prize winner

Raw Man
by Pulitzer-Prize nominee Fred Rivera
Winner of the Isabelle Allende Miraposa Award for best new fiction

This lightly-novelized Vietnam memoir, now required reading at major
universities, derives its title from the author's epiphany: "Twenty-seven
years after I got on the flight home, I saw that 'Nam war was just *raw man*
spelled backwards. I'm pretty raw today."

A Word with You, Vol. I
The best from A Word with You Press
An anthology of select winners from the literary contests of *A Word with You Press* from 2009 to 2018

Falling for France
by Nancy Milby

The first in *A Foreign Affair* series finds Annie Shaw having to choose between a successful career and real romance with a French aristocrat, and wanting both.

French Twist
by Nancy Milby

The saga continues as American archeologist Louise Marcel becomes entangled in nasty business on French soil, as she conceals her own hidden agenda.

Finding France
by Nancy Milby

The third in the *A Foreign Affair* series finds Gabrielle Walker lamenting a life unraveling, when a letter informs her she is the inheritor of a large estate in France. Then it gets complicated!

Finding Home
by Nancy Milby

Etienne, the recurring enigma in the series *A Foreign Affair,* is brutal to his enemies but a gentle giant to those he loves. Can the secret woman in his past enter his life again? Perhaps, but not with complications—some predictable, but some...

A Word with You Press
Publishers & Purveyors of Fine Stories in the Digital Age

Other selections are in the pipeline. Check back with us often, and visit
our online store at *www.awordwithyoupress.com*. Most books are available as
print editions and e-books. We have also a growing selection of gifts for
writers, and please check out our latest contests.
We'd love a word *from* you!

A Word with You Press
Publishers and Purveyors of Fine Stories
310 East A Street, Suite B, Moscow, Idaho 83843
www.awordwithyoupress.com